Tales of Illeross: Turning Point

ELLIE LERUM

RED RICHARD ARTS

To my dearest husband, Phillip, for putting up with me and everyone involved. I love you, I tolerate you, and I appreciate you.

Introduction

Tales of Illeross has been an idea for several years, ever since the first release of Jean Cassy and the Phantom in the Dark. We knew we were to write something, something so important to the work of the Kingdom, but we didn't know where to start.

Turning Point, the first book in the series *Tales of Illeross*, is a special book to both myself and my husband, Phillip. There are aspects of both of us in the characters portrayed, most notably the love between Flick and Anca; while I could fill several pages with information of how they're like us, and follow us, I'll refrain and only give this bit.

Without Phillip, my walk with God would not be right.

After many years of running from hurts caused by people who claimed to be 'Christian', it took the patience -or stubbornness- of a Follower of God continuing to ask me to church before I said 'yes' and regained the beautiful relationship I had with my Lord.

Much like Anca, Phillip pulled me from a delusion of being able to do it by myself, and I'm forever grateful for the patience and faith that he displayed both then and now. As for the remainder of the book, the theology, please be aware that it is not my intent to force you into hostility. My beliefs are my own, and I have done my best to represent those beliefs in a loving way for all who read it. If you do find that my words have bristled you, please know that it is my prayer that you know that you are loved despite whatever it is that you disagree with, and know that sometimes the most loving thing is to tell others where the cliff edge is.

This stated, please enjoy the love story not only of Flick and Anca, but Flick and a God who is very real, very tangible, and who very much wants to know you.

Ellie Lerum

Contents

CHAPTER ONE

Where Meetings Take Place

Some stories are stories of luck. Others are stories of fate. This one isn't quite either, as it is a story of faith and love despite a world that seems to be against all things different.

Illeross, a land of magic, and secrets, has many cities and people. One of them, Zanther, is the focus of this story. Within the bustling city, full of Solari worshipers and inquisitors who turn their faces towards the sun, a man is getting ready for work. It had been a long night and he, Flick Alastar, knew that the day would only result in more exhaustion. Rather than focusing on this, however, he instead looked at himself through the mirror and straightened his ascot. If he could just get his black hair to cooperate, he'd be able to use the shadow to hide the bags under his dark eyes. "Miss Rani?"

"Yes, Master Flick?"

"Drop's new medicine needs to be taken precisely at noon: any later, and I'm afraid that it will also be made null. Both of them have piano to finish. If it is easier for them to focus, they can complete their poetry in the rose garden." He glanced back at the nanny and raised an eyebrow.

"I won't be home until late tonight, so kindly get the children fed and ready to sleep before I return home."

"Yes, sir." The servant dipped her head as a little boy ran into the room. He was no more than three with dark, messy hair and wide blue eyes. Slowly following behind him, coughing quietly, was his slightly older sister. Unlike the boy, her cheeks were hollow and her eyes, though blue as well, were mostly lifeless.

Flick turned to see them. "I didn't think you'd be awake before I left... good morning, little ones." He caught the little boy, Shatter, and then held his hand out for Drop. "Have the two of you said your morning prayers, yet? Thanking Solaris that you awoke for the day?"

The children both shook their heads and Flick crouched with them. While they managed to follow along, it was he who murmured, "We thank Solaris for rising above this world and thus shining his holy light over us. It is a light that purifies the wicked and gives us our life; without it, the darkness would settle, and we would lose our way. We thank him for his cleansing fire and pray that we can please him in this life and the next."

Flick kissed his children's heads and then stood. "Listen to Miss Rani, I will be home to tuck you in."

"Bye, Daddy," Shatter chirped. Drop sunk into a chair with nothing more than a tired smile.

"Goodbye." Flick kissed their heads once more and rested his hand briefly on Drop's shoulder. She shuddered under the slight weight, making Flick's eyes soften as he removed his hand and turned away. "Miss Rani, my mantle is resting beside my bed—"

"I do keep forgetting you are a cote, sir... you haven't worn it in months. Why, I remember the first time I saw you as an avian and I nearly—"

Flick waved his hand at the nanny. "Yes, yes... I need you to get it to my father later today; he is doing repairs on his own and I need him to look at it as well."

"Do I need to do anything for the feathers?"

"Just be careful."

He looked over his little family and kissed his children once more before he left.

As much as he had wanted to stay, he had a job to do: it was his responsibility, after all, to provide for his children. It wasn't as though working as an inquisitor and the responsibilities that came with it made it possible to bridge home life with work, though, and in keeping the children secret— as well as his personal life— only made it more difficult.

Flick rubbed his forehead as he made his way through the busy streets of Zanther. While it took him out of his way, he was sure to walk past the grand citadel to press his hand against one of the prayer ambers. There, he whispered a quick petition for Drop's healing before he hurried through the merchant's quarter and towards the barracks located in the northern most section of the city.

He had to be careful even with that prayer: no one knew what position he held in this city, save for the High Council and a handful of other Inquisitors.

That is, the rest of the secret police.

He knew there was a position opening soon on the council; the coveted position of a High Inquisitor was going to be available for one individual to take once old Treatis died. Flick knew he was in the running, but it would also require a massive achievement to secure it... Such as turning in heretics.

Rumors had been buzzing about a group of Kingsmen, heretical worshipers of HaMelech the usurper, throughout Zanther as of late. Even more alarming were the reports that filled his office talking about strange meetings, magic that didn't come from Solaris, and an influx of people wielding the cursed glowing weapons of HaMelech. While it posed a threat to the safety of the city, it still proved to be a potential in ensuring that he, rather than any other Inquisitor, would receive the promotion.

Flick ran into someone, the shock of impact enough to send him to the ground. He blinked furiously at the sudden interruption in his walk before he realized that he was beside a pile of brown fabric and nearly white-blonde hair. In the center of the pile, a young woman wiped at her face to clear it of hair. "Goodness' sake..."

"I'm so sorry." Flick stumbled to his feet and then took the young woman's hand. "I wasn't watching where I was going. Are you okay?"

Guilt flooded Flick as he realized a slight bruise was beginning to form where he had hit her with his shoulder. The woman stared at him for a moment before she nodded and pulled herself up. "I am, thank you. Something must have your rapt attention to not have noticed me."

Her words made his cheeks grow warm. "No, I mean... I hope I didn't offend you in this—"

The woman laughed and, in an instant, Flick was smitten.

He smiled as she began to grin. "Offend me? Simply by not paying attention?" She shook her head and then brushed herself off. "You didn't offend me at all. I'm Anca, by the way, Anca Cassy."

"Flick Alastar."

"Flick, I like that name. It's different." Anca smiled before the bell struck. She glanced back and then sighed, "I'm so sorry to cut this meeting short, but I'm due to get to work—"

"You're working?" Flick asked, his cheeks growing warm again before he rubbed the back of his neck. "Sorry, that was a stupid question—"

"It's alright." The young woman chuckled softly again and then lifted her skirts. "Perhaps we could meet again, next time with less time constraints."

Again?

Flick nodded a little bit. "Yes, I'd like that. How might I...?"

Before he could finish his question, Anca's blonde hair was simply a part of the crowd.

Damn it.

Flick muttered under his breath as he began to follow her, simply a coincidence until she turned down a different street, and then paused briefly. Then, as a small crowd of people walked past him, he sighed and continued.

It took him no more than ten minutes to arrive at the gate house and stare at the imposing structure before he shouldered the oak and iron door open. A handful of guards glanced at him and waved before Jordon, one of his right-hand men, began to snicker. "Who did you meet, Alastar?"

"What're you on about, Jordon?" Flick sunk down at his desk and began to scan the map of Zanther. Given the street Anca had gone down, there were only a handful of potential options for her job. She seemed too innocent for a brothel; her hands were delicate enough for seamstress work...

"You're smitten."

Flick glanced up at Jordon to find that the man was inches from his face with a stupid grin.

"I'm what?"

"You've found yourself a pretty lass, haven't you? Give us the details."

With an eye roll, Flick went back to the map. "Her name is Cassy—"

"Cassy? I know that name... What was her first name, it started with an 'A'..."

"Anca?"

"That sounds about right." Jordon leaned back. "She works at the brothel just down the way, sweet gal, nasty temper if you cross her. I didn't realize you were interested in wh—"

"That's enough, Jordon." Flick looked up from the map. "I wouldn't expect her to work there."

"Blue eyes, pretty blonde hair, eyelashes that could sweep the floor clean?"

Flick frowned, his cheeks suddenly hot. "I didn't say any of that."

"It's her." Jordon snickered and stood. "Come on, how about after duty I go with you and you can try your luck with Miss Cassy, hm?"

"And where might you be going before then? You've got another four hours here based on what I scheduled." Flick raised his brow and looked back at the map.

"Back on my route. Come on, old man, why don't you come with?"

Flick shook his head again but stood with a snicker. "It's my turn to do 'paperwork', I'm afraid."

"Whatever you say, boss." Jordon slapped Flick's shoulder and then ushered most of the patrol out.

While Flick was alone, as the guard was either outside with Jordon or busy in a different part of the building, he put his armor on, took a deep breath and concentrated on his appearance. The steel of his protective gear began to shimmer and turn a pearlescent white while a hood formed over his head.

This was the Shroud of Solaris: unlike most inquisitors- Jordan included- Flick's personal armor was covered in an illusion that made him look like he was wearing the inquisitorial uniform. Most of the shroud merely darkened the hood, hiding the face, which allowed the inquisitors to act in anonymity. If Solaris's favor was particularly strong, as it was with the High Inquisitors, not only would the armor appear out of thin air, but it would be hard as steel without the wearer needing attire beforehand.

Pleased with his appearance change, as every inquisitor would take part in it to remain unknown to those around them, Flick stepped outside and joined the patrol.

As they walked through the streets, people parting to each side of the road as they caught sight of the guard and an inquisitor, the rank stench of feces and death filled the air. Flick detested the sewer district; it was close to the artificial river that had been put in while his parents were young and was where the waste of the city was swept away. There was more crime there than he preferred and of the people who weren't criminals, he hated having them ask for a couple of coins to get through the day.

There was little to do outside of breaking up a handful of scuffles while they walked, though one small child made the mistake of throwing a rock at Jordon. Flick watched, silently, as the group halted, and the boy was returned to his mother by the ear. While he wasn't close enough to hear, Flick knew full well that this was the first and only warning to the family about mistreating the Solari guard.

The group continued to walk after Jordon finished reprimanding the family, crossing through the sewer district towards the merchant's quarter. In the center, where Flick had passed on the way to his guard house, was the Grand Citadel of Solaris.

The citadel shone gold in the sun and the amber that had been added to the building sparkled, too. As usual, it was quiet and the few people who were there gave quiet, respectful nods to the patrol. Flick paused briefly to put a hand on one of the prayer ambers again. "Take care of Drop... and let me meet Anca."

They moved around the citadel, through the merchant's center, and then circled back to the guard house. By that point, Jordon was off and the remainder of the guards who were to patrol had caught up to them.

Flick found himself walking with Jordon towards the brothel in question after removing his armor and, as he did so, he could feel his throat tightening. It was one thing to look for a young lady through the town, another entirely to go to her place of work. A brothel, no less.

Jordon led him in. "Looking for Cassy, if you please?"

"Certainly."

Flick looked over the woman in front of them, who gestured grandly into the building for them to have a drink and rest while they waited. Then, she disappeared, and Jordon sunk into a chair.

"So, how interested in this girl are you?"

"Jordon, I don't want to discuss this... I also don't think this is a good idea; there are so many other ways to meet a girl—"

"Have a drink, then." Jordon waved to one of the other women and Flick watched as she gestured back at him. "Besides, you met your last two girlfriends in a bar, what's the problem?"

"It ended terribly the last two times I did this," Flick muttered, shaking his head.

"Then try lowering your expectations and just enjoy the ride." Jordon propped his feet up on the table. "If anything happens, you can pay them off; you're rich. And besides, this way you can get a test ride before deciding to pursue her."

Flick glared towards Jordon and tapped his fingers. It was then that he caught sight of a familiar blonde coming down the stairs towards them. Her icy eyes seemed to search his soul and, while Flick could recognize parts of her features, something seemed wrong. She made her way to their table and Flick did his best to stare at her face rather than her outfit or the assets she flaunted.

"I heard you called for me?" She questioned, putting one hand on her hip.

Flick stared up at her before Jordon spoke, "He's been thinking of you all day."

"All day, hm? And why, pray tell, have you been thinking about me?" The woman leaned down to stare at him, and all Flick could do was blink. "Cat got your tongue, mister?"

"You... aren't who I'm looking for," he stammered dumbly.

"Not..." The woman jerked back before her eyes narrowed into dangerous slits. "Who *are* you looking for?"

"Flick, I told you this was her," Jordon muttered. "Don't piss her off."

"You aren't Anca, my friend must have misunderstood—"

"Anca?" The woman's eyes grew wide, flashed with anger, and then narrowed again. "If you're looking for Anca in a brothel, I'm not about to help you find her."

She turned away from him and Flick, his mouth gaped, stumbled, "Please, I'd like to meet her again. I ran into her on the street, and she had to go to work."

"Anca does not work here, nor will she ever work here." The woman spun around, her nose nearly touching Flick's. "While I appreciate you attempting to follow up on this little... *adventure*... I suggest you stay away from her."

"Anc... Ad... babe, can't you give him a hand?" Jordon asked.

The woman whipped towards him. "And you, Jordon, are getting on my nerves. You brought him here and forgot my name, didn't you? That's the only damned way you could tell anyone that my sister worked here, and I didn't!" Jordon visibly shrunk as she continued, "My name is Adriata, before you forget again. I would have expected you to remember it after you've requested me each night for the last two weeks!!"

"Miss Adriata, please, I'd like to talk to your sist—"

"Don't you ever think of looking for her in here again," she interrupted before she shouted, "Get these two out of here!"

Before Flick registered what happened, he found himself on the street with a sore jaw and a nearly unconscious Jordon.

His friend groaned. "I forgot how nasty an arm she had when she got mad... Look, I'll see if I can dig anything up on your little girlfriend, alright? Adriata's sister... I have a way with women, I can figure out where she might be. And don't worry," he snickered weakly, "I won't flirt with her before you get a chance to say 'hi'." He slowly sat up, rubbed his face and then stood, "Anyway, I'm going to get home. See you in the morning, captain."

"Good night," Flick muttered.

The walk home was quiet, and he paused upon seeing Miss Rani in the parlor. "Did Drop and Shatter not go down?"

"Drop did, sir, nearly as soon as she was finished picking at her supper. She didn't eat much more than a few mouthfuls again." The nanny glanced at him. "She seems listless, and I'm not entirely sure if she'll sleep at all through the whole night."

Flick's heart sank, "Alright. You rest, I'll gather Shatter and put him down. Thank you."

He plodded into the house and collected his son. The little boy was more than pleased to spend some additional time with his father as Flick ate his dinner and then read quietly in the parlor with him. Flick laid Shatter down after several hours and then retired to his room to rest. As soon as his weary bones hit the mattress, he closed his eyes.

CHAPTER TWO

Where Secrets Are Revealed

He didn't think he would hear anything from Jordon until later that week, though the first thing he discovered upon entering the office was a stack of papers and a grinning Jordon. "She works at an infirmary here in town, she's 19, and she's a devout Solari like her sister."

"Why did you look into her like this?" Flick questioned, skimming over the paperwork and then putting it down. "I want to know about her through interaction, not by your stalking."

"You're welcome?" Jordon rolled his eyes. "She's working again to-day."

"Good, I'm not bothering her right now."

"Why not?"

Flick glared at Jordon from across the table. "I don't want to bother her at work, while I'm supposed to be working, and certainly not when I'd like to get to know her naturally, not with a stack of papers telling me everything about her!"

Jordon merely shrugged and Flick sighed. "You don't understand anything about women."

When evening rolled around, as Flick assumed Anca would be off work at that point, he made his way to the busy street that he had first met her on. Then he waited until a blonde came from the street he had last seen her disappear on. He waited for her to notice him first before he approached with a soft smile. "Miss Cassy, I'm glad to have run into you again."

This time, she was wearing a light green blouse and a pair of brown pants with her boots. Her hair was braided down her back and her eyes softened as she realized who he was. "Mr. Alastar, I'm surprised you remembered me."

She stopped to face him, and Flick smiled. "Well, I hope you don't mind my running into you again; I realized there wasn't any way I could have gotten to see you again outside of a chance happening."

Her laugh answered him, making Flick melt ever so slightly. "I'm glad to know I wasn't the only person to realize that."

"Well... I don't know what you're doing this evening, but I just finished working a little bit ago and I wouldn't mind getting you to where you're going tonight," Flick offered, holding his arm out.

Anca raised an eyebrow. "You're very forward."

"Would you like me to stop?"

"No, though I would like to refrain from physical touch; I don't want to cause anyone to think one way or another about either of us if we're seen together... People talk, and while I don't know your profession, I do not need my patients thinking one way or another about me."

Flick blinked at her before he lowered his arm. "I haven't heard of that before, but I won't argue. Would you let me walk you to your next destination?"

The young woman smiled towards him. "You know, I think I would enjoy that."

They set off silently before Flick mused, "So... What do you do for work?"

"I work as a nurse," Anca replied.

Her words made him smile sadly, briefly, before he looked away. "You must see a lot of things, then."

For moment, neither spoke before Anca murmured, "I do... But I think my purpose is to walk alongside those who are injured, or grieving, and give them a shoulder to cry on. But enough of the sad ideas; what do you do?"

"Me?" Flick started and then searched the sky. "I am on the city guard. Long shifts, long nights, but it pays the bills."

"So, you get to witness firsthand many of the things that send patients to me," Anca stated.

Flick blinked at her before Anca searched his face. "It isn't your fault, I know it isn't. I don't think you're the type of person to use police brutality on those you interact with." She stopped in front of a house and folded her hands in front of herself. "You know, there's very few people in this city who think that the fire of Solaris is better used on chitters than civilians."

Her words made Flick freeze and he raised an eyebrow. "That's a bold idea, Miss Cas—"

"Anca, please. No formalities, especially if you'd like to get to know me more." Anca waved him off slightly. "I'm well aware that it's a bold idea, but those ideas are the ones that change anything happening."

She stepped off her threshold and looked up at Flick. "And on that note of bold ideas, I think I'd like to hear your thoughts on the matter."

He stared at her before he murmured, "I think the fire of Solaris is used when the inquisitors feel that it's right and I have no say in the matter of when it's used. If there's any handful of reasons they might decide to purify; I don't want to get caught up in it."

Anca searched his face once more, nodded faintly, and then turned. "I don't know when you'd like to see me again, as you seem keen in doing so. I'm free in two days and wouldn't mind an evening walk—"

"Could we try to meet for a lunch instead?" Flick asked, shifting as he calculated how late he'd return to his children otherwise. "Then we don't need to worry about the streets when they get darker?"

His words received a soft smile. "Alright, lunch in two days then?"

"It's a date."

Anca chuckled quietly and nodded at him before she slipped inside the house. Flick watched her go before he smiled faintly. This would be nice.

He returned home to receive similar news to the last night; Drop didn't eat, she fell asleep quickly, but she was restless.

The next several days seemed to move too slowly for Flick as he waited for Anca to join him for lunch. She was in a light orange outfit as she left the infirmary. "Do you wear anything but black?" she questioned teasingly.

Flick looked down at himself. "I thought I looked rather professional."

"You look like you're a part of a wake." Anca laughed softly as they walked towards a small eatery. "How have you been?"

"Busy. The city guard has been dealing with some problems in the sewer district; there's threats of riots breaking out." Flick sunk into his seat. "A handful of people seem discontent with everything happening politically and they're trying to make things change."

"Hm." Anca sat across from him. "Well, there's no use clinging to what happened in the past. Why don't you focus on the now? You're eating lunch with a young lady, and you want to get to know her, I'm sure?"

Flick glanced at her. "And here I thought I was the forward one?"

"Can't I be as well?" Anca asked.

Her question made Flick smile and he shrugged. "If you want to be, I suppose. That does bring me to a question, if you don't mind."

"Yes?"

"I... Noticed that you're not wearing an amber prayer stone; did you lose it?"

Anca paused and then reached up to touch her neck as though she was looking for a necklace. "I suppose I did... You know how flimsy those chains can be; I must not have realized it came undone at any point."

"Aren't you worried that you won't be able to interact with him, then?" Flick asked quietly. "You seem confident in everything that you've said and done, and you're doing good work. How might you get your good deeds counted towards your ascension if you haven't had it replaced?"

The woman chuckled and shook her head. "No. I know He's with me wherever I go." She smiled ever so slightly. "I don't need a stone for Him to do that."

She really did seem to be devout, stating that she didn't need amber to interact with Solaris. It was intriguing, really, as Flick gazed at her. "Do you think that everyone should be able to interact with him—"

"Of course, I do." Anca giggled again. "That'd defeat the purpose of Him being God, wouldn't it, if no one could interact with Him?"

Flick nodded a little bit again before he changed the topic. "Do you enjoy working as a nurse?"

"I do. I like to be able to help people in the way that I was designed to; I love holding their hands to help them find comfort, or talking them through a fear that they overcome. I don't like delivering bad news, but at least then I can help support them." Anca took a bite of her lunch. "It's a hard job, but I enjoy it."

Her words made Flick smile ever so slightly as he murmured, "You sound like you care. We need more people like you in this world."

"You seem like you care, too," the woman pointed out quietly. "I've seen the look in your eyes as we walked together; there's a larger heart and a greater desire in you than I've seen in most."

They gazed at one another before a bell chimed and Anca sighed, "I suppose I should allow you to return to work. When do you want to see each other next?"

"I could walk you home tonight, and we could have lunch together again this week?"

Anca smiled a bit. "I'd like that."

Flick met her outside of the infirmary to walk to her home, where they chatted idly about life in Zanther and their families. Anca's parents, he discovered, were no longer around and she instead lived with her older sister Adriata. In return, Flick told her that he had a father and no mother. They also talked about the friends they had at work, like Jordon or Anca's close friends Marin and Catherine. Flick couldn't help but smile as Anca recounted the two women fondly, explaining that Catherine was a devoted mother who would bring her child to the infirmary from time to time to help Marin wash bandages or towels while Marin was the best healer she knew.

They stopped outside of her house and were near saying 'goodbye' when the front door swung open, and Flick found himself nose to nose with Adriata. Now that the sisters were near one another, he could see how similar they were despite their differences. Anca's curly hair escaped the confines of her braid and curled teasingly around her face while Adriata's straight hair was pulled back and up. One was curved as she wore a revealing corset beneath her robe while the other seemed more boxlike in her conservative suit. The most noticeable difference, however, was the scowl on one woman's face and the gentle adoration on the others. "Anca, who is this?"

"Flick Alastar, Miss Cassy. I believe we've met before, though in an odd circumstance." Flick stepped back, putting Anca between him and her sister. "I apologize again for that—"

"Anca, come inside."

"Adriata, wait. I was just saying goodbye to Flick when you opened the door. Have you met before?" Anca looked between them, raising one eyebrow, before her eyes landed on Flick. "Where did you meet Adriata?"

Before Flick could respond, Adriata snapped, "He came to my work looking for you, accompanied by one of my regulars who didn't have the decency to remember my name. On that note, Mr. Alastar, have a good evening. Anca, inside."

Flick glanced at Anca, rubbing the back of his neck sheepishly, "A friend of mine thought that you were her and was trying to help... Have a goodnight, I don't want you to get in trouble for staying out too late."

"Never mind her, Flick." Anca shook her head and briefly rested a hand on his arm. "I'll see you later, alright? Take care and have a good evening."

"Anca!"

The blonde smiled at Flick before she turned and went inside, leaving Flick alone as the door slammed. He couldn't help but smile despite having Adriata learn that he had found her sister, and the giddiness carried him home.

Upon opening the door and seeing Miss Rani in the parlor once more, Flick's happiness faded into concern and exhaustion. Yet again, Drop was doing poorly.

Several months passed this way; Flick would hurry home after walking Anca to her house, discover that Drop was doing no better than the previous day, he'd spend the evening with his son, and then join Anca for lunch the next day. It was exhausting, but the luncheons were a welcome break from the monotony of the day. If not for needing to finish due to work, Flick was certain they could talk all day. The conversations were also something he looked forward to, though they often revolved around faith and leaned more into heresy as Anca spoke to him. Still, it was good company and an even better way to spend his time.

Finally, after four months, Flick leaned back in his chair. "Anca?"

"Hm?" She glanced up from her soup, one blonde eyebrow delicately raised in curiosity.

"I've been thinking... We have been seeing one another, unofficially, for a while now. I was wondering if you'd like to, perhaps, make this more official? Say that we're dating, and use that in conversation?"

Anca began to spudder on her soup, making Flick blink at her before he slowly passed her a napkin.

"I'm sorry, Flick, you just startled me. Are you sure? I mean, I would very much like to see where this goes, but I also know that..."

"Know what?"

"Well..." Anca fell silent for a moment. "I know there are some things that we don't agree on."

"We can talk them through and come to an understanding," Flick said gently. "I'm not always right, we both know that."

"It's more than that, Flick," Anca murmured. "I just... This is going to take a lot of work, and I'm afraid that if I say the wrong thing, I'll ruin this relationship."

"I won't let that happen." The man offered her a gentle smile. "We can at least give it a try, alright?"

Anca opened her mouth to respond before footsteps moving hurriedly over cobblestone caught Flick's attention. He looked towards the street to see that one of the house servants was running this way.

Flick furrowed his brow; this wasn't something normal, especially during the lunch hour.

"Master Alastar!" the servant panted, his hands on his thighs as he stopped before them. "Please, come quickly! Miss Rani summoned the doctor already; he is on his way."

"What's happened?" Flick questioned. He could just see that Anca was watching intently, the faintest hint of concern on her face as the servant hung his head.

"It's Drop."

Flick's blood ran cold at the words, and he hurriedly stood up. "Anca, I'm so sorry but—"

"Let me come with, to help," Anca interrupted softly. "I don't know who Drop is but... If the doctor has been called, then you may need some emotional support."

While he didn't like the idea, Flick also didn't have time to argue. Instead, he gave Anca one short nod and raced through the streets towards his home. Anca's shoes clicked behind him as she ran after him before she slowed upon reaching the door.

Flick wasted no time in entering. He ushered Anca in quietly, took his coat and scarf off, and then hurried to the parlor.

"Miss Rani? Where's Drop? Has the doctor arrived?"

"Just moments before you did, Master Flick," Miss Rani whispered. "He's in the nursery with her. I have Shatter reading in here with me."

She gestured to the little boy sitting on the sofa and Flick instinctively checked him over before he hurried towards the stairs.

"Flick?"

He ignored Anca as she called after him and instead made his way to the nursery. Inside, Drop was pale and still on the bed, glistening from the sweat that covered her thin face. The doctor had placed a cool cloth over her forehead and straightened up as soon as Flick entered. "Master Alastar."

"Is she alright?" Flick asked quietly, making his way to the bed and taking Drop's hand. It was limp, though he could see there was still breath in her lungs as her chest rose and then fell. "What is it?"

"Master Alastar, I'm sorry to say but all you can do now is keep her comfortable; there isn't a clear answer to what has come over her and falling asleep like this. Comas don't tend to lead the patient to anything but Drisis and his gates of death. It pains me to say but I truly doubt that she'll last the week."

Flick blinked at the doctor and then sunk onto the bed edge beside his daughter. It was as though his world went numb in just a handful of seconds as he stared at Drop and then began to cry.

"I'm sorry, Master Alastar. I can prescribe some medicines to help with whatever pain she may be experiencing, but that's all I can do." He rummaged through his bag for a moment and then held out a small bottle. "Give her a few drops of this each morning; it'll help her relax."

"I don't need painkillers for her!" Flick finally managed. "I need you to heal her!" He swung his hand and solidly hit the bottle, causing it to clatter to the floor. "I've paid you a small fortune to help her, there has to be something!"

"There's nothing more—"

"Then you're not trying hard enough!" Flick stood from Drop's side and drew his sword. "You haven't done anything more than tell me that she's going to die! What use are you if you can't even heal a child!"

The doctor backed up, stammering, before a soft voice and touch caught Flick off guard. "Flick?"

Flick stood there for a moment, taking his time to register that someone had lightly put their hand on his back, and then looked behind himself. Anca stared up at him, her eyes wide and full of tears. The sight alone made Flick drop his sword and it landed on the floor with a clatter.

He looked away from her as she spoke. "How long has she been sick, Flick?"

"Two years, four months, and eleven days." Flick pulled away from her and returned to Drop's side as he spat towards the doctor, "You, get out of here. I don't want to see your face again."

He didn't look at the doctor as the man ran, nor did he look at Anca as she whispered, "I'm so sorry, Flick. If I had known that you had children—"

"Then you can leave as well," Flick muttered. "They are my family and if you can't accept them then..."

"Flick, please." Anca sunk onto the bed beside him. He could just see tears in her eyes as she looked at Drop, and she whispered, "If I had known that you had children, and that one of them was so sick, I would have asked for you to spend time with them instead of me." Her words made Flick glance at her as she continued, "If she's been sick this long, you shouldn't be spending time with me. She needs you; I don't want to take you from her."

"All I can do for my daughter now is pray for her and hope that if I do enough that maybe, just maybe, she'll be healed." Flick looked away from Anca and hung his head.

He hadn't done enough to this point, though, to earn her healing. He'd been trying for months now; double shifts, additional purifications, doing what he could to demonstrate Solaris' glory. None of it had worked.

Anca's voice broke him from his thoughts, "May I pray for her, please?"

"If you really want to."

Flick took his amber set ring off and held it clasped to Drop's limp, boney hand as Anca rested her hands on his. It was a light touch, light enough that their 'no contact' agreement was being kept in mind as Anca began to whisper, "Mighty King... We have come before You to ask for Your hand in this situation. Our abilities, our strengths, and our discoveries are too small for this sickness, and we know You are more than it. Grant this little one Your peace, be it through soundless sleep or the full healing of her body and give her father rest as well. We know that if she is healed then it's by Your will, and regardless of Your will we know that this is in Your hands. Thank you, Lord, for giving her such a loving father, and such a devoted family. Keep them close during this time and continue to bring comfort as You know best... Amen."

Her quiet prayer made Flick stare at Drop, his silent hope that Drop would begin to move or show any sign of strength. After a moment of looking at her, he finally glanced at Anca. "Thank you. I—"

"You don't need to say anything, Flick." Anca offered him a gentle smile. "I know full well how this feels, and how frightening it is." Her eyes flashed with sadness for a moment before she shook her head. "Just... why didn't you tell me that you had children?"

"Anca, these kids are all I have. Their mothers... I don't know where their mothers went, and to be honest I don't care. Drop was an accident and I found her on my doorstep; I couldn't turn her away. I fell in love in an instant. And then Shatter... I was stupid and I slept with another woman, and she was going to remove him before he was born. I couldn't let that happen, I knew it was my responsibility if she didn't keep him and..." Flick trailed off, willed his voice to stop shaking, and whispered, "You know how dangerous this city is, especially for people who follow the edicts. My job, the people I work with... Keeping my kids safe from them, and from anyone else who might use them to hurt me, is my main priority."

"Do... You think I'd hurt them, Flick?" Anca asked gently.

Flick stared at her, looked at Drop, and then looked at her again. "I don't think you'd hurt them, but I think you'd hurt me. Dating a person with kids is something that most women, at least the ones that I've interacted with, dislike. I figured there was something different about you. The irony is that I was planning on telling you soon just... Not at all like this. "

Silence answered him, and Flick lowered his gaze before quiet laughter filled the air. He glanced at Anca to see she was shaking her head and giggling despite the situation. "I'm sorry... I just... Anyone who doesn't accept your kids with you is someone who I think is best not with you. I'm glad you're willing to keep your children first."

She met his eyes and Flick blinked at the amount of gentleness he saw in her gaze before he whispered, "Well then. If you're willing to keep seeing me, would you like to have dinner with me later?"

"When?"

"Tomorrow?"

"I'm busy tomorrow," Anca mused, "But if you want someone with you tonight after the news with Drop, I can stay this evening; I'll need to send word to the infirmary that something came up, but it's been such a slow day that I'm sure it won't be a bother. I don't mind making your family something to eat, nor do I mind spending time with your son if you wanted. What's his name?"

"Shatter."

"Shatter," Anca murmured, beginning to smile. "I like that name. And her name is Drop?"

Flick nodded silently and watched as Anca placed a gentle hand on Drop's shoulder. "Hello, Drop. I'm Miss Anca, a friend of your papa's. He's taking good care of you. Get some rest, little one, you'll need it to heal up."

The slightest bit of movement answered Anca's quiet words and Flick's chest tightened before he carefully brushed Drop's hair from her face."She's a sweetheart... She'd probably say she likes your eyes; blue is her favorite color."

"Blue is mine, too." Anca glanced at Flick before she carefully stood. "That was their nanny downstairs, wasn't it? I'll see if she can point me to the kitchen and I'll make dinner. Unless 'Master Flick' has a chef, as well?"

"No, no, Miss Rani cooks for us." Flick shook his head. "Please, don't worry about it."

The young woman raised an eyebrow. "I'm going to worry about it, and I'm sure Miss Rani won't mind showing me where your cooking utensils are." She started to the door and then glanced back at Flick. "Besides, this is something that girlfriends do, isn't it? Take care of the one they love?"

Flick stared at her. "Alright. Thank you, Anca. " He let the smallest smile creep over his face again before he looked at Drop and simply held her hand.

Anca returned with two bowls of warm broth filled with potatoes and carrots. She placed one on the bedside table and then sat beside Flick with the other. "You focus on eating, I'll see if I can get Drop to eat anything."

"I can feed her, it's alright—"

"Flick, please let me help you in this way," Anca said gently. Flick was surprised to see how firm her eyes she were as stared at him. "You've taken care of these two alone aside from the help of Miss Rani, let me help you now. Focus on yourself for just a little bit; I can feed Drop and Shatter is with Miss Rani. Take a moment for yourself, please."

The man looked at his daughter and then at Anca. "If you're sure."

"I am."

He nodded faintly and turned away as tears began to fill his eyes. It'd been a while since he was able to really focus on himself; while he knew the kids had been safe with Miss Rani each day, there was something about Anca's presence with his children that soothed him more.

Anca left only after Flick had eaten his fill and Shatter had been taken care of for the night. While Flick insisted that she be walked home, the young woman declined and left on her own.

With that bit of time for himself, Flick lifted a shawl made of feathers and threw them over his shoulder. His form shifted and morphed to create a tall avian and Flick stretched out his arms. It'd been a while since he had been able to wear his mantle and it felt good to be in it.

Everything was stiff still, prompting him to lift one bird-like leg and then the other to stretch it before he carefully tended to the feathers.

This was something else that he wanted to keep secret from Anca, at least for the time being. Giving her the additional bit of information that he was a cote, alongside the fact that he had children, was too much for one sitting.

He wore his mantle for several hours, simply getting used to the avian form again, before he pulled at the feathers on his back and the mantle easily came off. Then, he laid down and slept.

CHAPTER THREE

Where Miracles Occur

F lick didn't go into work the next day, given that he only had so much time with Drop. Finally, though he was reluctant to leave his daughter with Miss Rani overnight, he was able to go for a walk with Anca.

They wandered around town for a little while before they settled by the lake. Anca seemed troubled as Flick looked at her; she was murmuring to herself with furrowed brows, though she didn't outwardly say anything to him.

"The Avatar of Solaris is lowering soon," Flick commented.

"Hm?"

"The sun is lowering. Anca, are you alright?" Flick asked, turning to look at her once more.

The woman sighed and stared at the sky. "If it's your will." she finally mumbled before she looked at him again. "Would... you like to join me for a gathering later?"

"Later, when?"

"Tonight, in an hour. It starts at 7:00."

Flick hummed quietly in thought. This could be any number of gatherings; it could be a Solari gathering, though he didn't know what would be happening that night, or it could be... It couldn't possibly be a Kingsmen gathering, could it? She had been saying things lately that didn't seem to be from a person who worshiped Solaris.

"I think I'd like that... but I don't want to be out too long; I need to get home to Drop." He settled against the bench again and then stretched. "Will Adriata be joining us? You know she isn't a fan of me."

Her laughter hit his ears and Flick closed his eyes to savor the sound as Anca answered, "No, she will not be. Friends of mine will be there, but not Adriata. As for how long it'll be, we should be home before 9:00."

They sat together for a little while before Anca stood and led them down the river towards the sewer district. Flick stiffened as they went further into the area, subconsciously moving closer to Anca. "This isn't a great place to be near dark, Anca."

"Trust me, Flick, it's alright."

He could just see her eyes as she glanced back at him before they ducked into a dark alley way and into a small, one-room building.

The first thing that he saw, something that made his heart stop, was a small banner depicting a three peaked mountain over a band of thorns: the symbol of HaMelech. He glanced at Anca, and she offered him a smile. "It's okay, they haven't discovered us yet."

"Oh, good," Flick choked in return.

She led him deeper into the building, closer to the banner of the Heretical Imposter King, before she sunk onto a cushion on the ground. Flick sat beside her and watched, silently, as others gathered and sat around them as well.

An old man, someone he remembered seeing in the merchant's quarter selling pottery, went directly beneath the banner and began to talk about holy texts and the Usurper. Anca listened, enraptured, beside Flick and all the cote could do was stare with a dry throat.

He had found them.

While this would be great for his career, he also had to keep Anca in mind; the blue-eyed woman beside him was supposed to have been a devout Solari, not an infidel. Something must have happened recently to shake her faith, that was all. Maybe, within the next couple of months, he could bring her back to Solaris and then turn the others in. Yes, that was the best idea. Then he could keep her safe, pursue a relationship, and become a High Inquisitor as well. So long as Jordon didn't catch wind of this, or any other inquisitors, it would work.

Suddenly, a pair of hands rested on his shoulders, and he looked back to see another couple had joined them. Anca exchanged a quiet greeting. "This is Flick, he's joining us for the evening."

"Welcome, Flick. We're glad that Anca was able to help you join us. Is there anything we can pray for you?" the aged woman murmured gently.

It took him a moment before he stammered, "One... one of my kids is sick. Sick enough that the doctors have given up. Nothing I've been able to do has really helped."

The older couple with him hummed. "Sick children are hard to watch; being unable to do anything is even harder..."

They lowered their heads, and Anca did the same. Flick, after a moment, looked down as well.

Everything that was said over him, the quiet petitions on Drop's behalf and the gentle thanks for Flick caring so much for his daughter, made the man feel both better about what was happening and sickened. The fact that they seemed to care so much about a stranger was almost heartwarming, but the fact that they believed so heavily that the god they served was a real, proper god did nothing but raise bile in his mouth.

Eventually, after several long minutes, the group disbanded and Flick found himself and Anca walking towards the river once more. He glanced at her. "How long have you known about their gathering?"

"Nearly six months, now." Anca pulled her cloak tighter around herself to avoid the chill. "I was fortunate enough to be told when I first joined the Kingsmen, by the woman who told me that I could be saved by His grace."

Flick hummed quietly. "So why did you stop believing in Solaris?"

"I... guess it just sort of happened. Each time I went to a Solari meeting, I felt more and more like something was wrong. There seemed to be a hole that I couldn't fill. I did try; I got more prayer beads, I spent more time at the citadel, and... Well, you know what it's like. It was as though Solaris' light had left. But while that was happening, I heard this strange, gentle voice calling my name. It only happened when I was quiet, like when I was meditating or focusing and had no thoughts. I didn't think anything of it as I knew Solaris was told to speak to us but... it was strange. I went to pick up my prayer beads and felt violently ill the moment I touched them. I ignored the feeling and the sickness went from just that to like electricity was popping and cracking through the air. I dropped them and then heard my name again. Naturally, as I had just dropped Solaris' prayer method, I fell to the ground in fear that it was Solaris before peace washed over me. The voice whispered my name once more and I had the strange desire to know more about whoever was calling me. It happened that a young woman serving with me approached later and I heard the voice tell me to speak to her. I did, and that's when I learned about HaMelech and His love for me." Anca smiled a little bit. "It's nice knowing that there is a love so great for me that I was pursued."

Flick offered her a gentle smile in return, unable to help his response despite not believing a word she said. "I'm glad."

What a strange concept. Gods didn't love, nor did they really save. He knew that, especially as an inquisitor. The fact that Anca had listened to those lies so heavily was concerning. "So, Adriata doesn't know?"

"No, and I don't want to tell her yet." Anca looked away. "I know she wouldn't understand; she is such a devoted Solari worshiper that... I'm scared for what'll happen to her once she dies, Flick... I'm afraid that her soul will be lost."

Her words made him stiffen and Flick glanced at her. "Yeah?"

"I don't know if she'll ever believe in HaMelech, or accept grace or Him and... Flick, don't you worry about your family?"

"My family believes strongly in their ideals," Flick responded instantly, "and I know my children believe what I teach them. I'm not worried about them at all."

Rather than the surprise that he expected to see on Anca's face, he instead saw gentleness and a fondness that he had grown accustomed to. "You're a good father for teaching your children, Flick."

Despite the honesty in her tone, Flick couldn't help but feel guilt stab through him.

He walked her quietly back to her home, paused outside the door with her, and then murmured, "Stay safe tonight, Anca, and rest well."

Her blue eyes seemed to search his soul before she murmured, "You too, Flick. Get some sleep."

While she didn't give him a kiss, Flick knew that her quiet words meant everything she couldn't do.

The plod home was long; Flick dreaded entering the house to hear that Drop was doing worse. He knew she was. Solaris had yet to heal her and the doctors... Well, they were useless, too.

He sighed, hung his head, and then pushed open the door. As expected, Miss Rani was waiting quietly for him in the parlor. "Master Alastar! I'm so glad you're home!"

"How did they get on, today?" Flick asked quietly, pouring himself a small glass of wine. "Is Drop doing any better?"

"That's the thing!"

Flick stiffened ever so slightly before Miss Rani continued."It's a miracle! Solaris must have heard your prayers; this evening, ever so suddenly, she woke up! Her fever broke, she ate what must have been her weight... She even cracked a joke at the table, I haven't heard her do that since she first became sick!" The nanny laughed. "She's an entirely different child, Master Alastar!" Her words nearly made Flick drop his wine glass as he stared at her, watching her giddiness bubble forth. "She's sleeping now, solidly, for the first time in weeks!"

"How... When did this happen?"

"No more than an hour or two ago, around 7:45? It was so sudden; Solaris is good!"

"Yes... He is... If you excuse me, Miss Rani, I'd like to go check on my children."

The wine glass was abandoned on his desk as he hurried from the parlor to the nursery and then crept inside.

Both Shatter and Drop were in their beds; Shatter had all but abandoned his blankets as he snored quietly while Drop, her body still thin and skin still pale, slept soundly. Flick placed a hand on her back and found that it was rising and falling without the rasping shudder he had grown used to.

Miss Rani was right; it was a miracle.

Flick sunk down onto the floor and stared at his children. He absentmindedly ran a hand through Drop's curly black hair, and then Shatter's short hair. "It wasn't Solaris... Solaris..."

He fell silent and then stared at the ceiling, blinking in the dark. Maybe it was just a coincidence? Maybe it was Solaris, and it was just a coincidence that Drop was healed, completely, when he had mentioned...

"It couldn't have been HaMelech," he mumbled. "He's a usurper... He doesn't care..."

Or did He?

Flick glanced at Drop, pulled the blanket over Shatter, and then stood up. He took just a moment to murmur 'goodnights' over them before he paused. "... Whoever is listening... Thank you... Thank you for saving my little girl."

CHAPTER FOUR

Where Executions Are Held

He met Anca the next day to walk her to work, silent until she asked how Drop was doing.

"It was a miracle. She was completely healed last night. She woke up in good spirits this morning, she ate, there was no coughing..." Flick trailed off, "I can't believe it, really."

He found Anca's gaze was on him with that gentleness again. She didn't say anything for several moments before she whispered, "I'm so glad that your prayer was answered, Flick. HaMelech is good."

Flick nodded mutely at her words. He didn't say much more before they arrived at the little infirmary that Anca worked at, when he finally asked, "How did you know she would be healed?"

"I didn't. That's why it's called having faith. I'll see you tomorrow." Anca ruffled his hair slightly and then stepped into the building.

All Flick could do was stare after her as a sad smile began to play at his lips.

Once more he trudged down the streets towards his guard house. Jordon was playing solitaire at the desk. "You're late, Alastar. You doing okay?"

"Of course, I am," Flick replied instantly, glaring towards him. "Why do you care?"

"Easy, friend. You simply seem troubled is all. It must be about finding those heretics, hm?" Jordon asked. He had looked up from his cards and then looked down again as though musing. "I know you want that promotion every bit as much as I do."

Sitting down, Flick ran a hand through his hair. "Mhm... And are you any closer to finding the Kingsmen than I am?"

"I have a couple leads; I'm planning on interrogating them in the next few days. All I need is a handful of minutes and Solaris' holy fire and they're sure to talk." Jordon snickered a bit and put his cards down. " You've been focusing on that pretty Cassy, haven't you?"

For a moment, Flick gazed at his desk. He studied the area he had gone to the church of HaMelech, and then where Anca was, before he looked at Jordon. "What I do in my spare time doesn't involve you, Jordon. However, the potential of planting a mole in the local whorehouses in order to get additional information aside from the usurpers is something that does. Adriata's a pretty face, isn't she?"

"Adriata? You're thinking of her helping you after she threw us out?" Jordon asked, raising an eyebrow.

"That's exactly what I'm thinking. We've got a place outside of town that she can take over as a mistress; she gives us information; we give her a nice place to live and a comfortable job." Flick leaned back in his chair. "No one would be the wiser."

He watched Jordon nod. "I suppose we can do that. I can get her collected and have someone make sure she's the right fit—"

"Don't use interrogation methods with her, Jordon. If we scare her a little bit, that's fine, but I don't want her to have any injuries or visible marks." Flick leaned forward. "I most certainly don't want to be involved with any of this."

"You're growing soft, captain."

"I'm covering my tracks... something that's required for a High Inquisitor."

Jordon snickered ever so slightly and stood up. "I'll get a handful of people together, then, and we'll make it look random."

Flick gave one short nod and went back to perusing the papers on his desk. He'd seen most of them, though he did pause in lifting one from the Council. "What's this?"

"I thought you'd know, since you're the one it's addressed to."

The letter itself was a formal one congratulating Flick on his current achievements, though he could see there was an underlying tone to it. It was more than just a congratulations and more of a thinly veiled explanation that he was in line for High Inquisitor... if things worked out.

It was, of course, signed by his father.

He blinked at the letter, looked up at the ceiling, and then back at the letter. This complicated a handful of things, didn't it?

Carefully, he folded it and placed it into his pocket.

A handful of reports came through later that day from silent, hidden messengers. Flick read over each of them and assigned them out before he paused. Chittering madness.

The haunting memory of howling chitters passed over him, their teeth glinting black with poison as they swarmed over villages, and he grabbed the hilt of his sword. *That* was something too dangerous to send his men to.

Without a sound, Flick pulled his heavy armor on, put his helmet over his head, and placed his sword into its sheath. He stared at himself in the mirror in order to manifest the Shroud of Solaris and then slipped into a backroom.

Beneath the rug was a hatch that only he and Jordon used; it led below the city to a vast network of tunnels. While the occasional civilian found them, it was a system mostly used by the inquisitors and High

Inquisitors for secret comings and goings. Getting to the city center and into the guardhouse there— the best way to remove suspicion for where inquisitors came from as they 'popped up' in places— took no more than five minutes. He then made his way into the streets accompanied by three guards who happened to be on duty. It was a safety precaution, something that was an unspoken agreement through those who joined the watch. With his small patrol, Flick made his way to the house in question.

The three men stationed themselves outside of the building as Flick let himself in.

Only a young woman was there, trembling in a corner as she mumbled about the darkness and eyes.

Flick stared at her, pity filling him before shame overwhelmed him. He was an inquisitor; he wasn't supposed to pity them! They were unfaithful people who had angered Solaris and were reaping the consequences for whatever sin they committed! He was supposed to enact Solaris' judgement on her! If he didn't, she wouldn't reincarnate with a second chance!

His blade lit with white fire and he approached the woman as she sobbed, "Please, please don't hurt me... They want to hurt me, please help me..."

Once more, Flick paused. Anca was getting to him, wasn't she?

"As penance for your sins, whatever they may be, that have scorned Solaris... I am here to enact your final judgement."

His steps felt heavy as he plodded to her, lifted his sword, and then brought it down. Her screams filled his ears for a handful of moments as he cut her down without a fight. As they died down, Flick stood still.

This felt wrong.

Tears stung his eyes and he crouched, unable to command his body to do otherwise. "I'm sorry..." he whispered. "I'm so, so sorry..."

The guilt that flooded over him made his knees weak even while crouching. After a few minutes of trying to compose himself, he finally stood and left. A crowd had gathered to see what the screaming was and it vanished as soon as he slipped out of the house. He didn't make a sound as he was escorted to a different building where he then entered the tunnels.

It was there that he sat and wept.

He wasn't sure why he was so affected by this; he'd put people down before and none of them, absolutely none of them, had bothered him. He was weak, that's what it was. He had grown weak in his service and, because of it, he was feeling guilty.

A soft voice in the back of his mind mumbled, *"Or you have a heart you've discovered."*

Flick took his time to return to his posting, his steps heavier than he was used to. The rest of the day was difficult to focus as the young woman's face kept flashing in his vision.

It wasn't until he picked Anca up, his girlfriend's eyes concerned, that he whispered, "I... I know we said no physical interaction... But can we make an exception, please? I... really need a hug right now."

Anca stared at him and Flick looked away, scratching the back of his neck before he felt Anca's arms wrap around him and her face rest against his chest. He instinctively pulled her close and pressed his face into her hair as he took a shuddering breath.

Finally, Anca whispered, "Rough day at work?"

"... Very. I think I need to take the day and be alone. I'm sorry, I know we were planning on dinner but..."

"That's okay," Anca murmured as she looked up at him. Flick was surprised to see that she seemed more concerned than upset by his words, especially as she said, "Take whatever time you need to process, Flick. If you'd like, we can have dinner tomorrow night instead. You don't need to walk with me to work, we can meet later. Is that alright?"

Flick nodded, took a deep breath, and then released her. "Thank you... You don't know how much I appreciate it."

He walked her home, and they said quiet goodbyes before he returned to his house.

Drop and Shatter both came running to him and he caught them. To his delight, and surprise, Drop was still doing well; she didn't cough, there was no fever, and as he sat down to eat with them, she ate more than she had in months. All Flick could do was hold them tight and think about what had happened the last two days.

It scared him, knowing that he was beginning to feel guilty about the work he did and that Solaris... Didn't hear his prayers.

It also scared him knowing that the High Council was aware of what he was doing. They'd be able to find his children if he wasn't careful, and that meant that they could find Anca, too. Neither of those were things he wanted, especially in knowing that Anca followed the Usurper and that her fate rested, currently, in his hands.

"Daddy?"

"Yes, Drop?" Flick murmured, looking down at her.

Her eyes were large and he couldn't help but smile as she cuddled closer to him. "Where's Anca?"

"Miss Anca is home right now, my love. She will be coming over in two days for dinner."

Flick pressed a kiss to her forehead as Shatter piped up, "Will she stay?"

"No, little one."

When Flick awoke, it was all he could do to peel himself from his bed and stare at himself in the mirror. He looked awful; between his sunken eyes and mussed hair, he looked as horrid as he felt what with tossing and turning all night.

He carefully got himself dressed into his best suit, carefully tying his red silk ascot before he pinned the Alastar family crest into the center,

pulled his suit jacket on, and then gathered his hat. He could hear Miss
Rani convincing the children to dress in their nice worship clothes, too,
as they prepared for a morning at the High Temple, but he didn't stop
to check on them. They would leave after he did, and not greeting them
made it easier to do so.

The carriage ride to the northern entrance of the Grand Temple was
uneventful and he stepped out carefully. The walk he took was a direct
path to the highly coveted central seating in front of the massive dais
where the High Priest of Solaris would give his teachings. It also gave
the most beautiful view of the massive stained-glass windows on the
southern wall that would capture the light of the rising sun and turn
Solaris' rays into a multitude of colors. On either side were the lesser
entrances, where tens of thousands of people of lower status would file
in to fill the massive stadium that wrapped around all but the southern
wall.

Miss Rani would have his children there, posing as their mother.

As Flick exited the long tunnel under the central seating, a massive
pyre with five wooden posts caught his attention. It appeared that
there would be a public execution today, given that the pile of kindling
and posts had been set up on one side of the dais.

Without much other thought, Flick moved down the rows of the
seating until he reached the Alastar family box. All but one of the seats
were covered in a thin layer of dust. Flick wished they took better care
of the box, given that it was almost 16 years since his mother died and
his father never joined given his own place of honor, but as he sat down
for his eight hundredth worship alone, the hope that perhaps Anca and
his children could one day sit beside him overwhelmed his disgust.

Before he knew it, the music in the temple swelled and Flick bowed
onto one knee. He raised his face towards the rising sun and rested
one hand over his head to join the tens and thousands of voices in the
chorus.

"I believe in Solaris, the Radiant king of the gods, and the five members of his divine council: Lunararia the north mother, Xolta the most high Inquisitor, Zephin the bountiful, and the traveling brothers Ireus and Drisis, may they guide our path through life and death."

"I believe in the cycle of purification through fire after death that with each life we live through our good works we may become the will of Solaris until he makes us part of his celestial kingdom."

"I will serve out Solaris' most divine will in my daily life by tithing to his church, by purging heretics wherever they may be spreading their poison, and by obeying the commandments of the high priests his most holy mouthpieces on Illeross."

After the pledge, Flick sat down to watch as one of the high priests walked up to the podium. Moments later, his voice thundered around the temple as he discussed Solaris' mercy in reincarnation, and the need for obedience...

A knock on the door to Flick's family box made him sigh and turn. "Enter."

The door cracked open and a figure wearing the pearly white armor of Solaris' Shroud, an inquisitor, shifted outside.

"What can I do for you?" Flick asked, raising a brow.

"One of the men who were going to take part in the execution tripped down the stairs; his leg is broken and—"

"And you need a replacement?" the cote finished, his brow still cocked until the inquisitor nodded. "Then lead on."

Flick donned the shroud as soon as he was out of the box, following his comrade into the inquisitorial tunnels that snaked their way through and to each part of the temple. There, he met nine other inquisitors. They stood in two lines of five with a flaming sword in both hands and wearing Solaris' Shroud: aside from height, they were nearly indistinguishable from one another.

Between each pair of inquisitors stood a figure beaten black and blue with enormous open wounds. They were dressed in little more than the irons on their hands and feet, a burlap sack that hid their heads, and an iron collar that was connected by a chain to the person behind them. Presently, two more inquisitors joined them as the front and back of the procession. They grasped the chains welded to the collars and the march began.

Just before they passed through the large door and onto the raised dais, they were joined by the final and most important member of the procession. An inquisitor stood before them, their shroud was gilded in gold, their blade adorned with inset stones, and whose mere presence demanded attention. Their status in the church and state was completely unrivaled, even by that of the highest priests: a High Inquisitor.

The High Inquisitor led the procession around the dais, parading the prisoners to the boos and insults of the crowd before they reached the pyre, and he raised his sword to the sky.

A sudden silence fell over the temple so completely that the buzzing of flies in the back row was audible. The High Inquisitor released his sword, allowing it to hang in the air as the fire running up its length reached hungrily towards the sky, before his gaze swept over the crowd.

"Good, devout, people of Zanther!" His voice echoed and, in an instant, Flick recognized that it was his father speaking. "Before you, today, we have five confessed heretics... Two of which are unsanctioned magic users." A wave of gasps swept through the temple before the High Inquisitor's gaze raked over the group, "Their very existence has been threatening the lives of your wives, and your children. So, good people of Zanther, what do we do with heretics?"

"BURN THEM!"

The High Inquisitor turned, grabbed his sword from the air, and brought it down onto the chain tethering the first prisoner to the others. The heat from the blade melted the chain and one of the inquisitors who had escorted him out pulled the bag from the prisoner's head to reveal a face completely unrecognizable through the bruising.

"Thaddeus Jensen! Unsanctioned mage using the heretical power of the Usurper and masquerading as a healer in order to curse the good people of Zanther!"

Flick's stomach turned as he watched the healer get pulled to the first post and hooked his collar to the post so that his feet barely touched the pile of kindling below him. That could have been Anca, if she wasn't careful.

"Elizabeth Wright!" The High Inquisitor continued after cutting the next prisoner's chain and the bag had been removed from her head. "Unsanctioned witch who used her powers to poison the minds of children and make even the most loyal dog bite their master!"

She, too, was led to a post before the two inquisitors took their position in line.

"Mr. James Conroy! A man who not only failed to protect his family from the call of the dark gods, but one who encouraged it!" A cry of rage swelled from the temple but was silenced as soon as the High Inquisitor raised his hand. "He harbored heretics in our midst and worked to make copies of their foul text!" As soon as the man was hung to the post, one of the inquisitors dumped a bag of loose-leaf papers onto the kindling at his feet. "This is what happens to those who try to spread the poison of the deceiver, the False King! They burn with their work!"

Next, was the woman in front of Flick.

"Mrs. Catherine Conroy." Flick's heart fell as he recognized this woman's name as a friend of Anca's, his stomach dropping to his feet as his father continued, "For harboring Heretics, and associating with unsanctioned witches, you should be sentence to death. But letting a child be poisoned by your unholy ways? Truly, you are the worst mother to ever walk Illeross."

As the woman was led away, Flick reached down to remove the bag from the head of the prisoner beside him. At first, he thought it might have been a young boy, but as he pulled the bag away to see shoulder-length red hair, he could see that it was a little girl no older than Drop.

"Little Annabell Conroy, whose mind has been poisoned beyond repair by the tampering of the dark gods and her neglectful parents, whose innocence was replaced with darkness, who was led astray by cheap tricks from their witches and deceitful ways. Let us all raise up a prayer for little Annabell's soul so that Solaris may yet be merciful; it was not her decision to be deceived. May Solaris the Mighty purge away the wickedness before it has a chance to permanently blacken her innocent soul and force her return onto this world as a curseborn!"

As the crowd boomed in prayer, Flick watched the little girl raise her head and attempt to spit on the High Inquisitor. It didn't make it far, but that didn't stop her as she attempted to cry, "I chose HaMelech! I was not tricked!" With the noise in the air, Flick was sure he was the only one who heard. His stomach tightened again as he led the little girl, the child Anca had once fondly told him about in discussing her mother and the help they gave at the infirmary, to the pyre. The other inquisitor and the one who brought up the rear stood at attention as he lifted Annabell to hook her chain to the pyre. It was too short, forcing her to hang several inches from the ground should he leave her there.

While asphyxiating would be better than burning to death, Flick knew the collar was too large and would do nothing but cause her more suffering during her execution. Without a sound, Flick carefully moved a chunk of wood for the child to stand on with his foot. As he did so, he noticed that the woman to his left, Anca's friend Catherine, was muttering in a language that he didn't understand. It flowed almost musically from her yet was unlike anything Flick had ever heard before.

He shook his head slightly, about to step back from Annabell as she repeated a line of Kingsmen text over and over about HaMelech's comfort while under the shroud of death, when Catherine stopped and looked directly at him.

"I... Forgive you, Flick," she wheezed, offering a weak smile. "HaMelech... HaMelech will forgive you too."

As soon as she spoke, Cathrine returned to murmuring in the unknown language and Flick simply stared at her.

He had imagined that, hadn't he?

He quickly stepped down to join the line of inquisitors to raise his sword at the mark of the High Inquisitor. After a brief salute to the rising sun, they stepped forward as one and plunged their blades into the dry kindling.

As the flames burned and licked at the legs and torsos of the heretics, the five souls lifted their broken voices in song to praise the name and goodness of HaMelech. It was an eerie replacement to the screams that so often filled the air at an execution, and Flick stood stunned as they praised the reason for their death.

It was quickly cut short as his father, the High Inquisitor, stepped into the line and caused the others in his way to melt to either side of him as fast as they could. Without a word, he plunged his own blade into the burning pyre and the flames jumped into an inferno.

The crackling and popping of the wood quickly drowned out the five voices and, after a final warning to any other heretic watching, the worship was dismissed as the smell of burning flesh filled the air.

Flick didn't think he would see Anca after the Solari worship, but after he arrived home and had a glass of wine to soothe himself after witnessing her friend's death, she knocked on his door.

Not a word was spoken as she let herself in and then clung to him, staring with wide eyes at the wall as he held her close and whispered condolences. Eventually, after several minutes of silence, she whispered her thanks and disappeared. She wouldn't allow him to walk her home, and Flick didn't see her until she joined him for dinner several weeks later as she sent him a letter asking for time to mourn.

It was something that made Flick wonder exactly how convinced she was that HaMelech was God, especially when He did nothing to save her friend. In fact, Flick was even sure that it could, in the grand scheme of things, make Anca realize how foolish she was for abandoning Solaris and thus help her realign her beliefs.

Finally, when she was feeling better, Flick collected her from work and walked her to his home. He helped Anca into her seat at the dinner table beside his own, smiling slightly as the right-hand seat beside the head of the table finally had someone in it once more, and then sat beside her. Miss Rani had prepared a thin vegetable soup for them to eat, though it was sparing that either Drop or Shatter took a bite of the meal as they pestered Anca with questions about what she liked or what she did.

Eventually, Flick excused Miss Rani for the evening- a rare occurrence- and ushered the small group into the sitting room to rest before bed. Drop and Shatter played together while Anca studied the handful of curios that Flick had collected while she drank a glass of wine with the master of the house. Flick kept her near as they had their after-dinner drink, one hand light on her upper arm as he used the other to carefully aerate his wine. Every so often, Anca would look up with a quiet question and he'd respond before Shatter ran to their side and tugged on Anca's sleeve. "Miss Anca? Can you read?"

Anca laughed at the question and pulled away from Flick, leaving him to smile fondly after them as Shatter led her to a small pile of books. She settled on the couch with Drop and Shatter on either side, prompting Flick to sink into his own chair and lift the paper.

After several minutes, Flick looked up to see that Drop's eyes were nearly closed while Shatter watched Anca read intently. They sat there together before Flick realized that both children had fallen asleep against Anca. She stood and gently laid them down on the couch.

"You know," she murmured, "I wonder what it'd be like to change forms like in this book. Cotes can do it, though..."

"Though?" Flick asked, raising an eyebrow.

"Well, they aren't that common, and I'm sure they wouldn't enjoy getting questions about their changing," Anca finished.

"It's called donning their mantle," Flick chuckled slightly before he realized that Anca was staring at him. "What?"

"How are you sure of that?"

With a sigh, Flick put his paper down. "There are some things that I haven't shared with you, and I suppose this is another one. I am a cote, and so are Drop and Shatter. They haven't received their mantles yet as they're too young."

Anca put the book down. "Can you show me?"

"Show you?"

"Your mantle, please."

Flick blinked at her, laughed, and then stood. "I suppose I can, Anca, but I do need to ask you to keep this a secret as well; I try not to let most people know about this, just like my kids. There's too many people willing to take advantage of knowledge like this."

"Of course, I'll keep this secret," Anca said. "I don't want you to be hurt, I'll do everything I can to keep you safe."

She received a soft smile as Flick reached for the black feathery shrug just by the fireplace. He shook it out gently, fixed some of the feathers, and then pulled it over himself.

In an instant, the familiar itching of feathers and scales flooded over him before he stood in front of Anca. She stared at him, he was certain she could see herself reflecting in his large, crow-like eyes, before she rested a hand on his beak. "This is amazing..."

"You think so?" Flick asked as he adjusted some of his wing feathers. "Last woman I showed thought I was a monster."

Anca paused at that and looked up at him. "I'm not her, though."

Flick stared at her, unable to smile despite wanting to. "You're right, you aren't her... And I'm more than fine with that."

He pulled his mantle off once Anca was done stroking his feathers and studying his limbs and then scratched the back of his neck. "I should take you home. If you get your things, I can put the kids down-"

"Why don't I do it with you before you take me home?" Anca asked gently. "Then you can say goodnight to your children and I can say goodbye."

Neither of the kids struggled as Anca and Flick lifted a child each and carried them up the stairs. Flick looked back to see that Shatter had cuddled into Anca's arms deeper than he had ever done with Miss Rani, prompting a soft smile from the man. They silently entered the nursery to lay them down and Flick kissed each of their foreheads. "Good night, Drop... Good night, Shatter," he murmured. "Sleep well, I'll see you in the morning."

He stepped back slightly and glanced at Anca. She was smiling at him, her arms folded lightly across her chest before she relaxed and murmured, "You're a devoted father... It's wonderful to see how much you've shaped them."

"Well, when you are the only caregiver aside from a nanny... Their entire life..." Flick sighed quietly and turned to face her. "Come on, I need to get you home before Adriata wonders where you are."

They were quiet on their walk. Anca bid him a quiet 'goodnight' upon reaching the door and Flick murmured it back. He turned to go before Anca caught his hand. "Flick?"

"Yes?"

"Please... keep safe after... after..."

Flick offered a sad smile and pulled her close. She pressed her face to his chest as he rested one hand on the back of her head and the other on the small of her back. "I will, Anca... Promise me that you'll be careful, too."

His girlfriend nodded slightly. They remained in an embrace for several moments before Anca gently pulled away and then went inside. Flick watched the door before he turned and hurried home.

CHAPTER FIVE

Where Betrayal Stings

Anca was unable to meet him for several days- Flick assumed it was due to the high number of inquisitors moving- but she did send a letter asking if he'd like to have dinner. Of course, after he met with her, they shared a hasty meal of bread and cheese by the river and then went together to a Kingsmen meeting.

The more Flick went, the more he wanted to know. Well, that wasn't entirely true. Each time he went to a meeting, he was given more information that confused him about the nature of the Usurper and His followers while he attempted to remember names and faces. The first time he went after the execution, for example, the message was about life after death. It wasn't a teaching about reincarnation, as he had grown accustomed to, but was instead about a new life and new Illeross that would be perfect; there would be no more death, or sorrow, or pain then. Anca took his hand at that teaching and clung to it, making him hold hers ever tighter as they broke into prayer groups and prayed for various people they called 'lost'.

The meeting after that was a message that was less of hope and more of a solemn message, "HaMelech knows the hearts of those in this city; He knows who will come to love His name and who will walk in darkness after shunning Him. All we can do is continue to pray for those around us that they may hear His voice, as we are unable to share it without risking our own lives."

"I would much rather join HaMelech than live my life in silence and fear," Anca said quietly.

Her words earned a laugh through the assembly and the old priest smiled at her, "May you live to see the day that you can share the word of HaMelech without risk of your life, dear child... He has called you from the darkness to do great things, and I hope that we may witness them."

"What happens to the people who don't listen to Him?" A young man, relatively new to the group as far as Flick could tell, asked.

The smile faded from the priest's face, "Then they will be turned away from our King at the time of judgement, and they will be tried and face judgement just as those who persecute us in the name of their 'god'. Even the demons they follow know that He is the True King, and yet the demons they follow refuse to allow them to know the truth. Solaris, the Black Dragon, Telfaria... All of them laugh knowing that those who follow them as their deities are sentenced to death at the throne of HaMelech, even if it is His will that they come to know Him."

Flick blinked at the man's words, trying to focus on the reason behind Solaris being called a demon, before the meeting was called and he was unable to retain the rest of the teaching.

On the third meeting, three weeks after the execution, Flick found that a goblet of wine and a small, rather flat bread were waiting beside the priest. Though he didn't understand what exactly was happening, Flick was silent as the priest lifted the goblet, "The night prior to facing the Black Dragon, the Dove blessed a cup with the creation of a new covenant, that His blood would be shed for His followers to free them from the wages of sin and death forever. Please, drink of the cup and remember His sacrifice."

The goblet was passed around and Flick, not knowing what else to do, lifted it to his lips as though to take a sip before passing it to Anca. After the goblet was back to the priest, he lifted the flat bread and murmured, "Likewise, He took the bread and gave thanks before He broke it. This is His body, which He laid down in our stead to take up the punishment for sin and death. Please, take of the bread and remember He Who Died for Us."

Again, Flick politely ate a piece of the bread as it was passed around, his brow furrowed as he studied the banner. HaMelech fought the Black Dragon? He had been taught that HaMelech did nothing of that sort, and that instead his followers summoned the Black Dragon due to not obeying Solaris...

"Master, where do the thorns come from in the sacrifice?" A young woman asked prior to the prayer.

Flick's eyes snapped to the priest as he carefully turned to the inquirer, "The thorns beneath the mountain, which symbolizes the Triune God of the Creator, the Dove, and the Breath, is a reminder of the crown that those who mocked our King gave Him. Rather than giving the Dove a crown of gold and silver as He deserves, being the Son of the Creator and the True King, we gave Him a crown of thorns to pierce His skin and make Him bleed.

"We know it was a part of the Plan of Salvation, the Great Sacrifice, as the shedding of His blood replaced the shedding of ours as He was perfect, but at the time... It was to humiliate him. We use it now to symbolize what He did for us, as a reminder that our God bled for us when we should have bled under His judgement..."

Despite his best attempts, Flick tuned out the rest of the answer as he tried to understand why a symbol like that would be used after it harmed their God. He sat there, so focused, that he didn't realize that he missed the final prayer until Anca lightly tugged on his arm, "Flick? Are you okay?"

"I... I'm fine, Anca," Flick answered, offering her a weak smile, "It's alright, I'm just tired is all."

He didn't realize how much he wanted to know until he had to miss a meeting due to a patrol, which he spent wondering about what the message was about and why the Kingsmen texts stated it as they did. In fact, Flick was so enraptured by the questions that had popped up with each meeting that he spent the entire evening prior to the Solari worship thinking, so much so that he woke up halfway through the service and had missed the entire beginning.

A knock on the door pulled him from his trance and he stumbled down the stairs to find that a messenger had been sent from his father. It was nothing more than a question of where he was, which Flick scribbled a reply that he was feeling ill and did not wish to spread it around the city.

After a fourth and fifth meeting, both holding Flick's attention as he tried to wrap his head around things and ask questions without being found out, he was met at the sixth meeting by a rather solemn priest.

"I received horrible news," the priest said quietly. Flick stared intently at him as he continued, "Brother Lawrence and his family, and all who were staying with him, had been discovered. The last thing we heard was that inquisitors had broken down their door. We can only assume the worst."

Silence responded to the statement and Flick couldn't help but feel nauseous.

That night, rather than just a teaching on how they would see their brothers and sisters again, they remained in prayer and agreed to fast as the Long Night was nigh. The priest lightly caught Flick's arm before he and Anca left, "Keep guard, my son; something is coming, something just as dangerous as the Eye of the Dragon. Keep up your guard and know that HaMelech surrounds you."

Flick nodded, weakly, before he walked Anca home. He had all but forgotten what time of year it was, prompting him to stop by Anca's door and lightly hold her forearms, "Be careful while the Eye of the Dragon is up," he murmured. "I know you've experienced it but... this time, well, I don't know if you had anyone waiting for you on the other side of the darkness, but you do now."

Anca offered him a soft smile. "48 hours of darkness, in which I can simply rest and feel HaMelech's power, is nothing." She gently brushed a strand of hair from her face. "I'm more worried for you as you're a part of the city guard; the Eye of the Dragon won't affect you with its madness, will it?"

"No, it won't. If I start to feel it, I'll seek healing. I'm more worried about the chitters that'll manifest than anything," Flick murmured. "Stay inside, bar your windows; I don't want to hear your name listed."

"You won't." Anca laughed softly. "Flick, in 48 hours the sun will rise and you'll see me again. I promise. HaMelech is good, the Eye of the Dragon has no power. Remember; He defeated the Black Dragon, He will rise again."

Flick offered her a little smile. "Alright, if you're positive. I'll see you once the sun returns."

Once he returned home, Flick checked to see that his children and Miss Rani were hidden in the safe room. There were several hours till the Long Night began, so he waited, sipping at a glass of red wine to calm his nerves before he eventually made his way to the southern balcony of his estate.

There, he watched the horizon as the first light of dawn slowly started to glow and thus silhouette the city's southern wall. As he watched, Flick pulled a leather strap to tighten the bracer on his forearm, copying the action on the other side, and finished donning his armor. A single ray of light peaked over the horizon as Solaris started his daily journey to shed light and life on all Illeross. Today, though, on the day of the spring solstice, this brought Flick little joy.

Flick sunk to his knee in prayer, whispering a hushed prayer of praise to Solaris, "Thank you for your light and the life you bring... Please... Please do not turn your back on us this year. We are a faithful people; we are an obedient people... We have kept your law, we have purged your city of heretics, please... Please do not let our city fall in darkness..."

Solaris slowly made his way up from the horizon and poured light over the city, illuminating rooftops but leaving the streets shrouded in darkness. Flick lifted his gaze to see that hundreds of others, like him, had begun their petitions while the light lasted in the south.

Flick's stomach grew tight as Solaris continued to rise towards the equinox. Maybe this year their prayers would be enough. Maybe they were good enough, maybe... No, he knew it was too much to hope for.

The light began to caress the lower section of some buildings as Flick held his breath. Maybe, just maybe...

Despite his hopes, darkness fell. It was like blinking and forgetting to open one's eyes, or the snuffing of a candle as nothing but blackness reigned over the city where there once was sunlight. Flick dared to look up at where Solaris had once been, at the exact equinox, only to find that there was nothing. And, though he did not look, he knew that there was the Eye that hovered directly above him. It was an eye darker than the darkness around it, and it was searching for his very soul as whispers began. They tickled his ear, whispering and pulling him to do terrible things and to act on his most primal instincts.

Flick shook his head to clear it as he stood. Though he didn't look around, he knew that people were fleeing from the rooftops to crowd around the pitiful fires they had painstakingly built to hide from the Eye of the Black Dragon.

His walk was slower, his hand light as he traced the walls of his home amid the half-working lamps. It didn't matter how much light they produced; they didn't light the halls as they should have.

An hour later, after another glass of red wine was drunk and a light meal of bread and cheese was had, Flick joined a patrol of guards while wearing his Inquisitor's Shroud. Each in his group carried a naked blade in one hand and a hooded lantern attached to a shield in the other. Again, just as the lamps in his home, the lanterns were only half as effective as they would have been on any other night. Instead of shining through the darkness, they only proved to add to the eeriness of the Long Night as they cast dimness into the black.

It seemed almost instantaneous that the sound of a chitter— a demon that looked eerily akin to a spawn of a rabbit and hyena— calling into the night was heard. Its cackle echoed through the streets and forced a shiver up Flick's spine as he knew that it would only grow worse from here: wherever there was darkness, there the foul spawn of the Black Dragon.

The patrol was on high alert as they moved through the streets. They put down chitters where they were found, totaling at least a dozen chitters who had yet to form a pack, but Flick knew their luck had run short. As they raced down the streets towards where most of the cackling chitters lay in wait, the sounds of fighting erupted amongst them.

Rounding the corner only made Flick's stomach drop.

Before them was a small sea of a writhing, chittering hoard. On the far side of the road, with their backs to the wall, was a group of civilians. Three brandished blades sheathed in light that cut through the darkness as they fought off the tide of monsters; Flick knew in an instant that they were Kingsmen as only they wielded such weapons.

With a cry, Flick's men charged into the fray. His own blade burst into holy fire and seared anything near enough for the flames to lick as he carved a swath in the chitter's ranks. As he spared a glance up, he realized that the Kingsmen were using this relief of pressure from the chitters to edge their way to the far side of the road, no doubt to put distance between themselves and the Solari patrol. One of them looked directly at him and, for a moment, Flick felt conflicted.

What if these were friends of Anca's, like the group he had executed? Would she come crying to him at the end of the Long Night, telling him that an inquisitor had cut down someone she knew?

"HaMelech help us, an inquisitor!"

The yelling of a Kingsman pulled Flick from his thoughts only to see that the group was now fighting harder than ever in order to break the engagement and run. Another scream filled the air and Flick glanced to the side to see that one of his men had been pulled into the mass of biting, bile-ridden bodies.

Anger began to swirl in his veins: it was these heretics' wickedness that brought about the Long Night each year. It was their fault that the chitters had infiltrated the city, that his men were at minimal injured while others laid dead.

With each thought, the flame along his blade grew brighter and hotter until even Flick couldn't stand its light. In moments, Flick had cut through most of the remaining shadow demons and his blade crashed into the Kingsman's hardlight blade with a shower of sparks. The Fire of Solaris licked hungrily at his opponent's blade, but the heretic's magic prevented his own blade from melting like butter under a hot knife.

"Run, I'll buy you as much time as... AHHHHGGGG!"

In three swift swings, Flick overpowered his opponent and plunged his blade into his chest. The smell of burning flesh filled the air and Flick leaned in. "May Solaris' fire purify your soul." With that, he twisted the blade further. With one smooth motion, he pulled the blade out in a wide arch, cutting down a chitter that had leaped to drive a bone dagger through his back, and then lopped the heretic's head from his shoulders.

As he turned to face the other five heretics that remained, a smirk covered his face.

They had made good on their friend's foolish sacrifice as they made distance, though one of them was screaming something and was being drugged by her companions as though she was attempting to reach the body that lay in front of Flick.

The inquisitor took a moment to look over his shoulder, watching briefly as his guards remained in combat with the remnant of the chitter swarm, before he looked back at the escaping group.

His guards would be fine without him.

Flick tightened his fist around the hilt of his sword and then took off after the Kingsmen, determined not to lose them in the vastly winding allies. He could feel the anger pulsing through his veins only growing stronger as he realized that the guilt he felt prior was due to their doctrine, something that had wavered his faith in Solaris and had most certainly ensured the Long Night would come. Tonight, he would prove his loyalty to Solaris by slaying these infidels, and tomorrow he would give Anca an ultimatum prior to turning in the list of names he had collected.

In a matter of moments, Flick closed the distance. His blade darted and wove between the two knights who yet stood, forcing them onto the defense as easily as it came.

He could tell that they were fighting his blade rather than him as their eyes locked onto the flames of his sword as it threatened to sear their flesh from their bone.

It was a rookie's mistake, something that the inquisitor was easily able to exploit even against these seasoned veterans.

The Kingsman screamed as Flick drove his sword into his shoulder, dropping the glowing short sword he had been wielding as he staggered back, and his friend charged with haphazard swings of his blade. The move saved the first Kingsman only temporarily as Flick took a step back whilst defending. With a single sweep of the leg, Flick landed a solid kick on the second man's knee.

His rival gave a scream of agony as the resounding snap of bone filled the air, making Flick grin within his shroud. Without another sound, Flick pulled his blade back to deliver the fatal blow.

Before he was able to swing, a shrill 'no' rang through the air. One of the women darted forward, her arms lifted over her head as though she was able to stop the flaming blade with her bare hands. Flick paid her no mind as he swung the sword down, intent on cutting through this heretic and finishing the fallen knight with a single stroke.

What he didn't expect was the sharp, sudden sound of metal on glass and a shower of golden sparks as his blade came to a complete stop. Between the Kingsmen and his blade was a thin, translucent shield, shedding a dim golden glow, that had seemingly appeared out of thin air by the woman's fingertips.

Flick leaned into the blade, gritting his teeth. This had to be some sort of unsanctioned magic, but certainly he could use his entire weight to drive the mage into the ground. Despite his efforts, the shield didn't move even as the woman took a half step back.

Now that Flick was unable to harm them, the slight fog in his head lifted and he took a good look at the people within the shield. He didn't recognize either of the injured Kingsmen, but the woman... She wasn't very tall, and the hood of her cloak had fallen back to reveal a mess of curly blonde hair piled atop her head in an attempted bun.

"Anca?" Flick choked out, staring at her through the shield.

Her blue eyes went wide and she took another step back, obviously applying more of whatever magic it was to the shield, and then she paused. Slowly, she leaned closer to the shield and then searched the darkness of Flick's shroud. "... Flick?" She dared.

In an instant, Flick's eyes grew wide and he forced himself upright, "I don't know who this 'Flick' is, woman. I am an inquisitor of the High God— "

"It *is* you! What... Wait... No..." Anca's face flashed through a mixture of emotions before she finally settled on anger. "Flick Alastar, you lied to me!"

Flick backed up slightly, glad for the shield between the two of them as Anca glared at him, before she stalked through the golden dome. "You never told me you were following Solaris, let alone an Inquisitor!"

"You never asked!"

"Why would I ask? The moment I said anything about being a Kingsman and you would have killed me... Like... Like you did to Terius! You killed my friend, Flick! He was like a brother to me and you MURDERED him!" Anca jabbed her finger through Flick's illusion and into his armor, her blue eyes alight with fury, "I brought you to our meeting places, I trusted you! I ate with you, I was your girlfriend, and you lied to me!!"

"This isn't what it looks like; you shouldn't be here, Anca. Get home, we can talk about this later-"

"Later?" Anca repeated, jerking her head back. "You really think there's a later?! Flick, do you understand how much of a problem this is?! I could get over the fact that maybe, just maybe, you were a confused person following Solaris. I could get over the fact that you were a city guard... What I can't get over, is that you are an inquisitor and that you LIED TO ME!" She pushed him and Flick stumbled backwards,."T here is no later! You had your chance before you did all of this!"

"All of... Anca, I'm doing you a favor! I didn't want you to be afraid, I was planning on telling you eventually but-"

"But nothing! This is it, Flick! We're done, completely and totally!"

Her words made Flick blink at her, helpless, as she continued, "We're no longer seeing each other, and I hope that HaMelech shows you mercy for what you've done not only to me, but to the people who I was supposed to keep care of!"

Flick blinked again, anger beginning to boil up, "You should have told me that you were going to be out here, then, as an illegal healer for them!"

"Don't you dare start, Flick Alastar!" Anca snapped, "I didn't tell you because you didn't need to know! Some comings and goings are between me and HaMelech and... And..."

"And I'm going to give you five minutes to run before I do something I really regret!" Flick roared back. He stared at her, his chest heaving. He knew she couldn't see that he was crying, and he was glad that she was unable to witness the angry, hot tears that streaked down his face. Neither of them moved before one of the knights grabbed Anca's arm and forced her away. Flick, rather than following them, turned and walked back to where he had left his guard.

In what felt like an instant, though he knew it was longer, everything seemed to be broken. His relationship with Anca, his ability to function, his desire to want to keep her safe... All of it faded away.

Flick gritted his teeth in order to steel himself as he reached his company and they continued their silent patrol. Any chitter hoard that they found was cut down brutally by the inquisitor as rage and guilt shrouded him.

It was eight hours of slaughtering chitters and running after Kingsmen, though Flick noticed that if there were any on the street they did a good job in hiding. He returned to the barracks for another 8 hours where he sat, silently, with his head in his hands. He had time to rest there, but rest wasn't something he wanted. In fact, as Jordon sunk beside him on the floor halfway through his break, Flick turned away from him.

"You should rest, Flick; it's a long enough night as it is outside of working 16 hours."

"I can't rest, I have to think," Flick responded quietly. "Leave me be, Jordon."

Jordon settled, silent for a moment, before he glanced at Flick again, "Are you and that healer seeing each other still?"

"Why?"

"Adriata mentioned that some 'runt of a guard' kept showing up at her home with Anca most nights," Jordon snickered. "You sure have a way with her."

"Shut up, Jordon."

"Come on, Flick, lighten up." Jordon nudged the other man and Flick, without looking at him, narrowed his eyes, "What'd you do to make her angry with you? You won't talk about Anca, what'd you do?"

"I said shut up, Jordon."

"Live a little."

"That's enough!" Flick finally snapped, whipping around to stare at his friend.

Jordon's eyes had gone wide at the sudden movement, his hand reaching for his sword, "Flick, the Madness hasn't gotten to you, has it? What have you been doing to react like this? An inquisitor shouldn't be so volatile..."

Flick glared at Jordon before he looked away, "She broke up with me, alright? She dumped me, and I'm angry. Now, I'm done with this. Leave me be."

"Touchy..."

Jordon was lucky he was out of reach, else Flick would have strangled him. Instead, the cote settled further into his misery and stared at the wall. It was his fault that Anca dumped him, and maybe that was for the best. At the same time, though, she did lie to him about being a healer... What were they called... A Dove.

The fact that Flick knew this information, even the simple title of a healing Kingsman, made him sick to his stomach.

Solaris would hand him to the chitters if he continued to think about the Kingsmen. Instead, Flick folded his hands and bowed his head to focus on praying to Solaris. While it would have brought him comfort any other day, the sick feeling only grew alongside a feeling of disgust and betrayal. The words he was saying, all his praise to the sun and the purging fire, felt like a lie after he had heard so much about a God who saved and loved rather than condemned.

Before Flick knew it, his time to rest had ended and he was forced onto the streets once again. The 8 hours were brutal as he hadn't eaten or rested, and many times Flick found himself struggling to remain awake or entirely focused. All he could do was walk alongside his patrol and sweep his flaming sword through the hordes of chitters.

The one time he found Kingsmen, while his guards were around, Flick merely gestured to them to give pursuit before they were lost in the alleys. Aside from that, Flick ignored the heretics. Each time the thought to go after them came to mind, Flick nearly doubled over due to the gut-wrenching agony that spiked through him and let the infidels run. Finally, after 24 hours, the sun rose from the darkness and the Eye of the Dragon was gone.

CHAPTER SIX

Where Choices Are Made

The sun was still weak as it rose above the city, though Flick didn't spare any glance as he made his way home. As soon as he had a chance to sit, with a glass of red wine, he pulled a leather notebook from his desk. Inside, scrawled ever so painstakingly, was a description of the old man who had prayed over Drop's healing. A sketch of his face was beside the description, as were notes on where Flick last encountered him. The next page was that of the woman who had prayed with the man. Following that, the merchant who Flick had met while disguised in the meetings... And finally, Anca.

Flick stared at the page as overwhelming grief flooded through him. If he had been honest, this wouldn't have happened. He tore his gaze from the page and let it linger on his desk drawer again. Without a sound, he opened it and pulled out a small black box.

He didn't dare open it, not for several moments, before he finally sighed and leaned back with it. He popped it open to inspect the dainty ring that was nestled upon red velvet; while the little diamonds adoring the band were beautiful, the larger ruby in the middle caught the firelight in his study as he turned the ring over in his hand.

"And to think... I managed to convince my mother to leave me this in her will," he muttered, offering the empty room a dry laugh. "She thought I'd propose to a noble Solari girl... instead, I was going to propose to a heretic."

He stopped short, guilt consuming him as he focused on the ring again. Was she worth more than the position on the council?

The question nagged at him as he sat there, looking at the ring and then at the notebook that he had spent so long taking care of.

She had been nothing but gentle, loving, and kind; the children loved her, and she loved them. He loved her. There was warmth from her... Solaris had no warmth. Solaris was not warm, and so far, Solaris had no power in his life. Drop wasn't cured by Solaris, but the god that Anca worshiped. The Kingsmen were protected and loved: all Flick could remember was fear and anger.

As Flick thought of this, the hatred towards himself began to grow stronger. If he hadn't been selfish, then Anca wouldn't have told him it was over; it was all his fault... No, it was his stupid devotion to someone who didn't care!

Before Flick registered what he was doing, he flung his notebook into the fire and watched it burn. His chest heaved for several minutes before he sunk down and simply cradled the ring. "Oh, Anca... I'm so sorry... What have I done..."

"Perhaps you should have asked yourself this before making the choices you did."

The new, unknown voice made Flick tense and, after he slowly paced the ring back into its case, he lifted his eyes to see that a man was sitting on the other side of his desk. One leg was crossed over the other as he folded his arms over his chest, regarding Flick from his seat with keen green eyes and a stern expression. "You have had enough time to have thought through what you were doing, and while there isn't much time left as far as I'm concerned, you have time enough to make a choice."

"Who... Are you?" Flick asked, his voice trembling despite his intent. "I've seen you before, at the HaMelech gatherings. You..."

"I decided to distance myself from you in order to raise suspicion should you have seen me elsewhere," the man interrupted. "My name is Osmond, and before you ask any additional questions about what it is I'm doing, I'm here on an assignment and have brought you a rather important message."

"If not for my Master, and His forgiveness when even forgiveness is not deserved, I would have struck you dead the moment you killed one of His children. Furthermore, had you decided to leave this house with the notebook you so violently burned, you would have sealed your fate and would have been dead before you could cross the block. However, as I said before, my Master is King and He forgives even people like you. He knows what your next steps are, and I suggest you begin to think through those steps before you decide to take any."

He stood up, making Flick flinch, before he paused. "Remember what you learned in those gatherings, Flick. You saw me there, which means you heard what you need. My King will always turn bad for good and will never allow good to be turned for bad." He reached out an open hand and Flick, after several moments, took it. The stranger pulled him to his feet and then turned away. "Move quickly, Flick; time is not on your side."

With the cryptic warning, he stepped towards the door and then vanished within a spark of light. The only thing that remained of him was a small, floating orb of white light that, after a moment, disappeared as well.

Flick stared after him and then looked at the ring in his hand.

If the Kingsmen spread the word that he knew, they'd all be in hiding. Anca, most certainly, would be removed from her home until further notice as she had spoken to him directly, which meant there was little way to talk to her. Unless...

Flick glanced towards the window and shielded his eyes from the blaring glare of Solaris, and then looked down at the ring in his hand. It'd take time, but he'd be able to at least try.

Without much time to waste, Flick riffled through his desk until he found a parchment and quill. Once he had, he began to write a quick letter, nothing fancy at all, that he then sealed with the Alastar crest. He stood to leave hastily, caught sight of a feathered shrug laying abandoned on the chair he had tossed it on, and then sighed, "Come here, old friend..."

He pulled it over his shoulders, embracing the warmth and sensation caused by feathers and scales covering his body once more, before he carefully left his home.

All he needed was to find a Kingsman that he recognized. They'd never seen his mantle before, providing him... The merchant's quarter! Flick broke into a run as he realized that he had seen a familiar face in the merchant's quarter before: an old man peddling even older clay jars. The cote ducked around a corner, panting slightly as he looked around the street.

Where was he?

It felt like hours before Flick finally caught sight of the man cleaning his stall. The ancient man's eyes darted around as though looking for something (Flick knew it was for Inquisitors) before they landed on Flick. "I'm sorry, I'm closed-"

"I don't need pottery, I need you to deliver something for me," Flick returned, stepping closer. He pulled the letter from his bag and held it to the man. "It is for a young woman named Anca... Anca Cassy. She was placed into hiding after the Long Night; I need you to get this to her." The man stared at Flick, uneasily, and Flick leaned in close, "You are Kingsman, I know you are. Please, find a way to get this to Anca."

"No, sir... No, I am not..." the man stammered.

Flick looked around, realized a guard was approaching, and then lifted a vase. "Three coppers hardly cover the cost of this work. I can do a silver, instead, for your time and effort."

As soon as the guard passed, the old man whispered, "How do you know who I am?"

"I've seen you at the meetings," Flick said, "and while I am not a friend, this secret is safe. Regardless, I need you to find Anca and give this to her. It is the most important thing, now, that you can do for me."

The old man offered him a little nod, took the letter into his apron, and then took the silver that Flick held out. "I will get this to Miss Anca as soon as I can."

Flick gave him a smile back before he found that the vase he had been holding was still in his arms and the man had turned away. "Sir-"

"Keep it; HaMelech guide you," the man murmured, looking back at him, "Go."

The words were cryptic, but Flick didn't argue as he made his way through the streets and back to his estate.

It seemed lonelier inside, though he understood Anca's presence was only here and there, as he placed the vase on his desk. The man allowed himself to slowly move up and down the halls, wearing his mantle, until the pattering of little feet raced behind him. "Papa, Papa!"

As he turned, he was met by both Shatter and Drop. They flung their arms around him and he rested his hands on their heads, stroking through their hair and savoring the touch of his children. "Sh, not so loud..." He sunk down to look at them, searching their light eyes with a soft smile. "You seem excited."

"We saw Miss Anca!"

Flick paused at the words and then pulled his mantle off. "When?"

"Just now! She was coming up the walk!" Drop pulled on Flick's arm. "Please, can we see her?"

Despite the hope that surged through Flick at the woman's name, he frowned and then shook his head. "No, Drop... Not for a little bit."

Honestly, he wasn't sure who was coming up the walk, but he knew that it wasn't Anca. It hadn't been long enough for the letter to get to her, and it most certainly hadn't been long enough for her to even want to forgive him. A rap on the door made him pause and he stood. "Go play in the nursery."

"But-"

"Now."

He ushered the children behind him and then made his way down the stairs. He could just see the top of someone's blonde hair through the peephole, causing him to draw in a breath, before he opened the door.

There, not quite paying attention to him, was Adriata. She was dressed in all black and was holding herself as she waited. Flick could see tears were filing her eyes as she watched the rose garden and then turned, jumped, and composed herself upon seeing him, "Where is Anca?"

Flick stared at her for a moment, "What?"

"Anca. My sister, you know who I'm talking about. Where is she?"

The man shook his head. "She isn't here, Adriata-"

"You must be lying! She was with you last, before the Long Night, and now she's gone! Where is my sister?!"

In an instant, Flick's eyes widened. Anca must not have returned home after they ran into him; Adriata hadn't been told what happened, where Anca was, or that she was safe. As he stared at Adriata, he suddenly realized that the woman was struggling to keep from crying and, though he knew they didn't get along, he sighed. "Come inside, Adriata; sit down and take a moment."

Adriata glared at him but, after she dabbed at her eyes, she stepped inside and into Flick's sitting room. He kept the door open and helped her into a chair where he then poured her a glass of wine. "Anca didn't come here with me. I dropped her off at home and said goodnight, and then I left her. She was inside the last I knew."

"So... So, she must be..." Adriata's hand trembled as she held the glass, her blue eyes wide and glassy. "My sister... They're going to read her name as an unfaithful; Solaris must have reincarnated her soul..."

"Adriata, if there's one thing I know about your sister, it is that she is the most devout woman that I've ever met. I know that she's okay after the Long Night, I have no doubts of it," Flick reassured quietly. "She's brilliant, she's resourceful, and she's diligent. Perhaps you missed her before she went to work? She holds fast to her responsibilities, and being the day after the Long Night..."

"She would have left after saying something, though..." Adriata lifted the wine to her lips and gulped it down, staring at her glass. "How are you so sure that she's okay?"

"Because I trust her, and I know that she wouldn't have done something so reckless as to leave your home unless she knew she would be safe," Flick murmured. He met Adriata's eyes and offered her a little smile. "You did a good job taking care of her when you were younger, she's grown into a brilliant young woman."

Adriata nodded faintly and set the glass down, holding onto herself, "I suppose I did... I still hope you know that I don't approve-"

"Adriata, I know. Which is why everything is up to Anca now. We... Got into an argument, and there is a good likelihood that she won't want to speak to me again whenever she goes home," Flick interrupted. He shifted a bit and sighed, "Whatever the case... Anca is wonderful and I know that she's okay."

The woman in front of him didn't reply and Flick lifted his gaze to see that she was glaring at him. For a moment, Flick was concerned that she was going to hit him before she murmured, "Anca cares about you. I don't know why, as all I can see is another selfish man behind your flattering… But I also know that I trust her judgment and I know that you make her happy. Please, if you hear from her, let me know."

"Of course… And… If you see her before I do, let her know I'm sorry," Flick said quietly. "I know she's okay, I just want her to know that I'm sorry."

He didn't receive an answer from Adriata as she left, though the woman didn't slam the heavy oak door behind her.

Flick remained in his chair for several minutes, staring at the wine glass and then the vase on his desk. He didn't take much time to look at it before, prompting him to lift it and turn it in his hands. That was a funny man in the market. Hopefully, he would get the letter to Anca.

CHAPTER SEVEN

Where Sins Are Forgiven

Life continued for three days as normal. Each morning, Flick would watch the sun rise in the distance from his balcony whilst giving a half-hearted prayer to Solaris. It didn't feel right to pray to Solaris, not when he was uncertain about his faith, but it didn't feel right talking to HaMelech, either. Instead, Flick muttered under his breath thanks for the sun rising to whoever it was that listened before he continued as before.

Jordon continued to bug him about Anca, though Flick ignored him, and each night, while tucking his children into bed, either Drop or Shatter would ask when they would see Anca again.

Flick didn't have the heart to tell them that they fought, so he would simply murmur, "I don't know, little one. Miss Anca is busy, and I do not want to distract her from her call."

Finally, on the fourth day, Flick was in his study working on papers when Miss Rani knocked on the door. "Master Flick?"

"Hm?"

"Someone is here to see you."

"Send them in, then," Flick replied, his eyes fixed on the document in front of him.

While donning the Shroud of Solaris was something he could still do, he had done what he could to do paperwork instead. It wasn't exactly an idea he wanted to follow, but more of one he had to follow as he had discovered something problematic; while going to purge a man with chittering madness, Flick's sword wouldn't ignite with flames.

He had tried several times amongst the begging of the ill man before he finally had to resort to simply running his sword through his victim's chest cavity. Amid the blood, Flick struggled with his sword three more times before he left the house. Even in his own home, where he had amber throughout the building, he struggled to get even a spark from his sword.

It scared him, but he couldn't say a word. The moment any other Solari found out that he, an Inquisitor, was unable to use the fire of Solaris was the moment that he would be put to death for treason.

Miss Rani's footsteps echoed as she returned to the room, this time followed by someone else. "In here, dear..."

Flick paused as a quiet 'thank you' answered the nanny and he slowly looked up.

Standing in front of him, wearing a white blouse tucked neatly into black pants, was Anca. Her hair had been pulled into a messy braid behind her head though the telltale curls around her face had escaped again.

As she stood there, Flick set his quill down. "Anca, I-"

"Who else knows that I'm a Kingsmen, Flick? You have your notes, I'm sure; is this a gathering prior to a public execution, where you'll light me on fire?" Flick flinched at her words, avoiding her gaze as she sunk down in the chair before him. Her hands, though shaking, folded delicately in her lap in a sort of poised, expectant way. "Or are you planning on asking me to give you more meeting places, names, and faces that you can collect to light ablaze with me? What's your game, hm? Perhaps you'll offer me freedom in exchange for those I know?"

Flick put his head in his hands, taking a moment to compose himself after her painful interrogation, before he finally sighed, "Anca... I'm sorry."

"What?"

The surprise in her voice stung him to his core but he continued, "I'm sorry, Anca. I'm so, so sorry that I lied to you and hurt you and... You'll likely not forgive me for a long while, if at all. I wanted to apologize to you in person before you left the city; I know they're going to move you, likely to Blackrock, and I wanted to see you one last time before you go."

He could feel her eyes burning into him as he sucked in a breath. "I don't know what to do, or what to say. I... I burned my notes. I got back after the Long Night and everything I noted, every name and face, I threw into the fire. I don't know what's happening to me Anca. I don't know why I am so torn about this; I don't know why I'm frustrated with myself... My sword won't ignite, I'm not even sure what I believe about Solaris and I'm supposed to serve him...

"I know I hurt you, and I know that all of my actions and..." Flick's voice caught and he sighed once more. "Anca, I'm scared. Anything that I do will result in you or the kids paying for it and... I can't do that."

He didn't lift his gaze, afraid that he'd see Anca leaving, before something gentle rested on his shoulder. He dared to look up to see that Anca had crouched in front of him to search his face. "What are you scared of?"

"... I'm scared of what's going to happen to me when I die, Anca," Flick breathed. "I went to enough meetings with you...Enough services... to know that you believe that people who don't follow HaMelech don't reincarnate. I'm scared that... Maybe that's right, and everything I was taught about Solaris was a lie. What if there isn't anything after we die? What if there isn't anything for my children after they die?"

"Then you also heard it enough times that HaMelech is calling people to follow Him and have a life after death that isn't reincarnation but is instead an eternity with Him, Flick," Anca murmured. She found his hands and Flick clung to her. "I've seen a change happen in you; you're not the man I first met. Something has been working on your heart and you're beginning to see that you're broken-"

"I don't want to be broken, Anca. I only feel guilt and shame and-"

"And that is HaMelech working in you to bring you closer to Him. He wants to make you like Him; mended and whole. Flick, there is no condemnation in love. HaMelech doesn't require any sacrifices aside from the life you live now in place of a new life with Him. He doesn't require you to slaughter people who don't fit your ideals, He calls you to love." She fell silent and then slowly reached out to lift his chin. "Do you trust me?"

"Do you trust *me*?" Flick whispered. "Anca, I lied to you about every-thing-"

"Flick, answer my question; do you trust me?"

He nodded silently and Anca allowed her forehead to rest on his own. "HaMelech help us..." she whispered, "I know you're struggling Flick... He does too. If you trust me, then let me take you to where I know you can continue learning the truth."

"What if the other inquisitors find out?"

"Then they do."

Anca closed her eyes and Flick did the same, savoring her touch as he whispered, "I'm so sorry, Anca. Please, if you'll forgive me-"

"I already did, Flick. I forgave you a little while ago, before I came here. I needed to make my peace before I was executed, and so I did. Now... I want you to meet me near the Sewer district later tonight, near 9. Bring the children, all of you in your mantles. I know you don't want them wearing them yet, but this will keep your family from being seen by the city guard and knowing your faces. I want you to join me for a service; please, just trust me on this. I don't know why I need you to come tonight, but I do. Can you do that?"

"You want me to show up to a gathering of Kingsmen after they know I'm an inquisitor? Anca-"

"Do you trust me, Flick?" she repeated.

Flick swallowed and then nodded, "I do. Are you sure this is a good idea, though?"

"I'm following what HaMelech is prompting," Anca whispered. "Honestly, I'm not sure if it's a good idea, but I do know I need to be obedient to Him."

Flick looked at her and shifted. "It sounds a lot like inquisitors and Solaris."

"It does... But this is obedience out of love rather than requirement. I could disobey all I want and, while there are consequences for what I do, HaMelech will still want me." Anca stood up and helped Flick. "Bring the children with you; just trust me and trust HaMelech. I don't know what's in store, but I know that it's a part of His will."

"I hope you're right."

It was nearing 9 o'clock when Flick was approached by Anca. She was shrouded in a dark cloak and she offered one to Flick as she closed the distance. "It's a late meeting tonight, I'm sorry. Are the children alright?"

Flick shifted Drop and Shatter both. They were covered in inky black feathers that helped them blend into the shadows, more so as they slept solidly against his shoulders. "They're exhausted but they're doing alright. I'm not certain why you had me bring them, as they could have slept at home."

"Neither am I, Flick." Anca gently took Shatter and held him near. "All I know is that you all need to be here tonight. Come on, we're going to be late."

He followed her as they went down the street and, eventually, they entered a building. The meeting was smaller this time as there were only four others who were praying quietly. No one looked at Anca and Flick as they entered and they instead began to talk quietly.

"We'll need to return to hiding, I fear," the usual priest said. "An inquisitor has been identified and he has seen us. HaMelech knows what will become of this, and all we can do is pray that we will be safe before we are called to His side."

Flick glanced at Anca and she looked at him in return as someone, a young man, spoke up, "If we know who it is, why don't we try to silence him?"

"Because HaMelech knows his heart and we are not the ones to cast judgement in his stead. Works do not define a person as much as their faith, my friend; while the inquisitor has done things that we shudder at, HaMelech's grace will cover him if he accepts it."

"Would HaMelech's grace cover an Inquisitor, though? They kill many people who don't deserve to die! Just a few months ago, my cousin was killed for chittering madness," the young man said quietly. "HaMelech can't possibly cover that."

Flick stared at the man as the speaker flipped through a book resting in his hand, the Holy Text. "I'm so sorry that you're speaking from a place of pain, child. The Holy Texts tell us of HaMelech's love and the Greatest Sacrifice. We know that the Sacrifice was made for anyone who was unrighteous, and we also know that none of us are righteous. We're all sinners, we've all done something that is evil in the eyes of HaMelech regardless of how 'good' we think we are. We're also told that HaMelech's Sacrifice created righteousness in whoever believes in Him; He took our place by being put to death and, because of it, accepting that atoning gift saves us from the fate that has been determined for those who turn away from Him." The old man was quiet for a moment. "While an inquisitor has done things, horrible things, HaMelech also forgives and loves His children should they ask for the forgiveness and love they're offered."

"Can't we do enough to earn that forgiveness and righteousness?" another individual asked.

"There are many questions tonight, all stemming from what happened, I've no doubt. No, my child... We are unable to do enough to earn forgiveness and righteousness; would a person who betrayed you be able to fully remove the hurt and pain that they caused you, even if they work on it the entirety of their life? Would they be able to do that if they keep hurting you while attempting to fix their mistakes? It is the same with HaMelech. Works may make us feel like we are able to earn it, but we must realize that the relationship we have with HaMelech comes from His extension of forgiveness and righteousness. It's a gift, you do not work to earn gifts as it's given."

Tears began to fall down Flick's face as he found the courage to speak up, "What... Would he need to do to be forgiven, and to... to be saved?"

He didn't expect everyone to look at him, especially as the older man stared at him for several moments before he answered, "Just like everyone of us have done, my child. Recognizing our sins, repenting them, asking forgiveness, and inviting HaMelech to enter our lives as we surrender our old selves to make way for a new life. It's creating the relationship and allowing HaMelech to shape our lives, doing our best to get to know Him through the Holy Texts while doing our best to follow His words in our daily comings and goings."

The old man stared at him for a moment longer. "I haven't seen you in any of our meetings before. How did you hear of us?"

Do you trust me?

Flick wasn't sure whose voice it was, as he knew it wasn't Anca's, but it was enough for him to close his eyes and then remove his mantle. The collective sounds of panic filled the air before Anca's gentle voice cut through the din, "Please, stop. Let him explain himself."

"Then explain." The old man stared at Flick again. "Why are you here?"

"I... I don't know." Flick looked at Anca, tears still streaking down his face. "I don't know why I'm here, but I know... I know that everything that was said tonight were things that... I don't understand, and I want to."

"We can't trust that," the first speaker, the young man, snapped. "Your type kill us for no reason aside from hatred. You're murderers... And you let him in again, didn't you? He found us the first time because of you, Anca!"

The group suddenly seemed to realize she was there just as Flick shifted closer to her. He kept Drop near as she slept, his other hand on Anca's back in order to pull her behind him should the crowd become violent. "None of this is Anca's fault. I'm the one who... Who tricked her into bringing me here. If you want to be angry, be angry at me. Otherwise, I want to know what I can do to be saved."

His words seemed to frustrate the young man, but the older man with the book stared at him. "HaMelech has melted your heart."

"Please," Flick said quietly in return, "help me to accept Him."

He watched as the old man looked at him, and then Drop and Shatter, before his eyes landed on Anca. "This doesn't have anything to do with interacting with a young lady, does it?"

"Only in the fact that she's done her best to help me figure things out," Flick said quietly. "I... I care about her, but I also hurt her and I know that time is the only thing that can repair what I broke. I am not doing this for her, I want to do this for myself and my children."

"Are you certain?"

"I'm positive."

Flick shifted a bit as the old man stared at him for a moment more and then closed his eyes. "HaMelech wishes to know you, child. Speak to Him and begin to form that relationship."

"How do I do any of that?"

He glanced at Anca as the young woman leaned into him ever so slightly. "It's like talking to a friend, Flick. HaMelech is the greatest friend we can ever have... It's talking to that quiet voice, not expecting anything verbal back, and resting in the knowledge that you're going to be heard by Him regardless of where you are."

"I... Don't need a prayer stone?" Flick asked quietly.

His friend's eyes softened and Anca murmured, "No... No, HaMelech doesn't need a silly rock to act as a messenger between you and Him. Here, give me your ring; it'll do nothing but add confusion to your mind as you try to understand how it works."

A small nod answered Anca and Flick carefully, slowly, pulled his amber ring off. "Are you sure? You know that the ambers help with Solaris-"

"HaMelech is nothing like Solaris, Flick," Anca said softly. "Now, close your eyes and give praying a try."

Flick glanced at her before he shut his eyes. He could see the swirls of color that painted the back of his eyelids as he simply sat and then whispered, "Are you there?"

Nothing answered him, but the slightest bit of comfort seemed to fill him as Flick took a deep breath and continued, "I... Have done so many things in my life that deserve death. I am a murderer, I lie, I steal... I've hurt people I... I love. They say You forgive Your children, and that You love them regardless... And I... I don't think I've ever wanted something more. Please, add me to your fold; protect me, guide me, teach me... Help me to understand why I have a purpose here. I... I need You, and I need to know that... Know that You are able to forgive me for everything I've done."

He didn't receive an answer, not that he was expecting one, but he did continue as the feeling of comfort lingered over him. "I was told that Solaris was the way, and that the things I did would dictate my life but... All of that is a lie, isn't it? I don't know where to go. I need... I need You."

He was suddenly aware of different hands resting on his shoulder or back, the feeling enough to make tears begin to fall down his face as he choked out, "You healed my daughter and brought her from the brink of death. Surely, you are the True God."

In that moment, it was as though a spark ignited within him. It was something that scared Flick but, at the same time, brought a sense of peace as he held Drop close and then rested a hand on Shatter's back.

I am with you.

Those few words broke Flick and he began to openly sob, hanging his head as he sat there. The small group of Kingsmen around him kept their hands on his shoulders and then a gentle hand rested on his cheek. With a sniffle, Flick looked up to see Anca was now in front of him, still holding Shatter where Flick could keep a hand on his back.

Her blue eyes were soft and she searched his face. "You heard Him, didn't you? You heard HaMelech's voice."

Flick managed to nod and the priest from before spoke, "You have a journey ahead of you, my friend. It is your job, now, to raise your children to know HaMelech's truth. Just know that you are not alone; though we must be in hiding, we are here to aid you."

He rested his hands on Flick's head and prayed over him, quietly, in a tongue that he didn't recognize. Anca's quiet voice joined in, speaking in a different language all together, before they fell silent and drew away from Flick.

A couple of people glared at him, still, but the gentleness and love that Flick could see in the eyes of the remainder of the group over-shadowed it. The meeting was called and Anca helped Flick carry his sleeping children home.

As soon as they stopped at his door, and Flick took Shatter from Anca, the young woman stared up at him. Flick shifted a bit. "Anca, I-"

"Sh, Flick," Anca said quietly. She searched his eyes, making Flick look away, before she murmured, "You're an idiot, I hope you know that."

"I do... I'm so sorry for everything that I did to you, Anca."

"I know," the woman replied, "and I forgive you. I'm busy tomorrow, but maybe, the day after, we can have lunch or dinner together again."

Flick smiled a little bit. "I'd like that, if you're certain you're okay with it."

Anca's nod made him smile further and he looked down at his children. "Drop and Shatter missed you, and I did too. I... Thank you for being willing to try this again."

"I trust HaMelech's will, Flick, and that includes whatever happens between us." Anca smiled at him before she kissed Drop and Shatter on the head. "I'll see you in two days-"

"Are you going home to your sister?" Flick asked suddenly, remembering Adriata's beseeching plea after the Long Night, "Have you been home?"

His question made Anca stop and she slowly lifted her gaze. The sadness that reflected Flick back at him told him everything he needed, and he murmured, "She is worried about you. When you didn't return home after the Long Night, Adriata came looking for you here. If it's safe to return home, and I hope it is as... Well... I was the danger, then please, go see her."

"... I will."

Flick watched Anca slip into the darkness before he turned away and entered his home.

CHAPTER EIGHT

Where Vows Are Exchanged

It took several weeks for he and Anca to mend their relationship to the point where they were both comfortable; Anca admitted that, while she was angry with him and hurt, she was also angry with HaMelech for not warning her. They commiserated over it for a few days before Flick asked if she'd consider dating him again, and she agreed.

Of course, there were many Kingsmen meetings that Flick attended either with her or alone. He found himself drawn to the word of HaMelech and actively sought it out, going so far as to procure an illegal copy of the Holy Text to read it secretly by night when he was home.

It was the eve of his mother's passing that he invited Anca to dinner, rubbing his neck. "I... don't enjoy dinner alone on this night; it's an evening full of memories, and even the company that I do have is less than pleasant."

"How so?"

"... My father dines with me. It's the only night of the year that he seems to want to do that, and I try my best to keep the kids from him as... He isn't the best person in the world."

"None of us are, Flick," Anca reminded gently. "He raised you; he can't be that bad."

"I was raised by a nanny, like Drop and Shatter. At least... As they are partially. I'm here for them, my father was not here for me."

His girlfriend rested her hand on his arm. "Well, I'll be there with you tonight and you won't be alone with him." She smiled up at him, only partially easing his nerves, and then leaned into his side, "Besides, I suppose it'll be nice to meet your father and see how you grew up-"

"Then I need to warn you to keep your tongue. He's in a higher position than I am, and while I don't think he'd be able to tell that we are Kingsmen, I don't want to risk it," Flick said quietly. "I don't want to risk your safety."

"I'll be fine."

Flick sighed and nodded, resting his forehead against hers. "You're right, you're right... How about I see you around 4:30, we'll expect him at 5. Wear something nice, please, as he expects it to be a formal dinner after we lost her."

Anca didn't disappoint him when she knocked on the door to his home several hours later. Flick nearly lost his breath as she handed Miss Rani her cloak to reveal a conservative yet elegant purple gown that draped over her form and highlighted her blue eyes. As soon as Anca saw his reaction, he blushed and looked away amid her soft tease, "It's no different than what I usually wear."

"No, but today I get to see you as Anca Cassy fresh from home, not work," Flick replied, laughing as she slapped his arm. He kissed her forehead and inspected her. "You do look lovely, Anca... Really."

"Stop," Anca murmured.

They shared an embrace for several moments before Anca pulled away. "Let me see if Miss Rani needs any help; I know I've got this dress on, but an apron will keep most of the flour off of me."

"Just no hugs if you get covered in flour; my suit can only show so much grime." Flick smiled as he watched her go.

She rejoined him in the sitting room for a glass of wine when the door gave a resounding shudder as someone knocked on it, making Flick pull in a breath and stand. "That would be my father. Anca, would you like to join me?"

Flick took Anca's hand and led her to the door. He took a second, deeper breath, and then pulled the heavy oak door back to reveal a man who stood even taller than he did. The man in question had streaks of gray running through his dark hair, his dark eyes held a wicked cunning and his face bore a handful of wrinkles, though none were from smiling. As soon as the door opened, his gaze snapped to Flick and then the young woman beside him. "Good evening, Flick... And his guest."

"Father, this is Anca Cassy," Flick said lightly. He pulled Anca a little closer to his side as his father's gaze landed on her. "Anca, this is my father, High Inquisitor of the Council of Zanther, Right Hand of Solaris, Fernando Alastar."

"It's nice to meet you, sir." Anca stared at Fernando before she looked up at Flick. "Why don't I see that Miss Rani has finished preparing the meal, Flick?"

"That'd be wonderful." The younger man offered her a smile and watched her go before he looked at his father. "Can I take your coat?"

"I'll keep it on, Flick." Fernando stepped into the doorway and made his way down the hall. "Where'd you meet her? Is she a cote?"

"On my way to work, chance happening. She isn't a cote, but we've been going to worship together; she's beautifully devout." Flick followed his father. "The kids love her-"

"I'm sure they do. Are you planning on asking her to marry you? You know how I feel about those with... Less than perfect blood marrying into the family; we're a proud family of raven cotes, and I do not want our line sullied." Fernando stopped and looked at him, his gaze unwavering as Flick straightened up.

"I am going to ask her to marry me, even if she isn't a cote, and I'd appreciate if you don't say anything while we eat as I really, truly, would like to keep a surprise."

Fernando scoffed slightly, "Keeping it a surprise... With your mother, I simply commanded her by my side and she did."

Flick bit his tongue as his father stared towards the kitchen and followed behind the other man as he entered the dining room.

The table had been set nicely for three, with a fish fork beside the standard dessert and main course cutlery and spoons of three different sizes resting on each side of the plate. Anca set down a tray with homemade bread as Miss Rani finished serving the soup. As soon as Fernando entered the room, the nanny gave a curtsy and then ran. Anca sunk into a seat after Fernando did and Flick, under the table, took her hand.

"Thank you, Solaris, for this meal which we receive. Your light is the one that shines through the days, purifying those who oppose you as you claim your kingdom; may your rays fall upon us and bring us justice."

As his father prayed, Flick's stomach turned and the feeling of vomiting overwhelmed him. It was something that forced him into squeezing his eyes shut, hopefully helping him to hide the fact that he wasn't Solari by being 'devout' in the prayer.

Anca, ever so gently, squeezed his hand under the table.

The meal was eaten in silence, something that didn't surprise Flick in the slightest, before his father looked at Anca. "What do you do for work?"

"I work as a nurse, not far from where Flick serves," Anca said quietly. "I'm still training, but those I work with are good to me and are very knowledgeable."

Fernando nodded faintly, took a bite of the meal, and then fixed his gaze on Flick. "I assume the two of you will be speaking to the head priest at the temple eventually?"

Anca glanced at Flick, who stared his father down. "Maybe we were going to, but I think a smaller temple would be more fitting now."

"Go to the high temple; anything you need, I suppose I can get for you."

"I don't need anything from you, and I never have," Flick retorted, tearing a piece of bread into two and then buttering it furiously. "Don't bother helping now."

"Flick," Anca said quietly, "just let him-"

"You certainly didn't claim to need nothing after your mother died, Flick."

Flick stiffened and he gritted his teeth. "It wasn't as though you gave me anything at that point, anyways; you left me with a nanny no more than 5 hours after my mother's body was removed and the blood from the dagger was cleaned."

"It made you stronger."

"I witnessed her kill herself!" Flick stared at his father, disgust rising as the older man simply smirked. Anca's eyes were on him as he finally whispered, "You can say it made me stronger as much as you want, but we both know that isn't what happened."

"You're correct; you became a sniveling excuse of an inquisitor," Fernando said, taking a bite of his meal. "However, the Council is pleased with your work. They investigated your deeds and, should anyone on the Council happen to leave their position for whatever reason, you'll likely be summoned to replace him... Or her."

"What?"

"And now you're hard of hearing. I said that you'll be summoned to the citadel should one of the other Council members leave their position." Fernando rolled his eyes and took a sip of wine. "Honestly, you'd think that you'd pay more attention..."

Flick fell silent through the remainder of the meal. His father idly talked about his job, Flick growing up (the words 'selfish' and 'cowardly' were used more times than Flick could count), and then about the Kingsmen insurgents. "Have you gotten any further in finding them, Flick?"

"I've a couple of leads, though I'll have to admit that Jordon has made more progress... And even then, he hasn't presented anything solid," Flick said, taking a drink of wine to steel his nerves. "One minute we get some sort of news, the next there's nothing there."

His father gave a soft sound, mostly of annoyance. "Then set your guards to patrol more often. This is getting out of hand, Flick. They're going to rise against the city before we know it."

"Of course, I'll do that as soon as I get to work tomorrow."

His father left shortly after that. Flick shut the door, locked it, and then sunk to the ground. "Go to the high temple..." he sighed and glanced at Anca. "I'm sorry, I should have known better than to attempt this."

"It's not your fault." Anca sat down beside him, her voice soft as she took his hand and held it gently. "He... Seems like he's the sort of person who does that." She was quiet for a moment. "I'm sorry about your mother. I didn't realize..."

Flick shrugged slightly. "It happened years ago. I should probably let go but... I don't know." He stared up at the ceiling. "Would you want to get married to me once all of this calms down?"

The sudden weight of Anca's head on his shoulder made him glance at her. She had her eyes closed as she leaned against him, her voice soft, "I'd like to get married to you whether things calm down or not. We both know that... Well, it's impossible for things to fully blow over as a Kingsman."

A little smile answered her words and Flick just kept her close. Eventually, after several long minutes, he pulled the little black ring box from his pocket. He shifted away from Anca just enough in order to see her face as he opened the box, revealing the ruby as it shone lightly in the oil lights. "Well... Then I guess now is as good a time as any.

"I've hurt you, and I lied to you, and you still forgave me. You've decided to stay by my side despite my shortcomings and all that I was before knowing HaMelech. I'm still a broken man, Anca, but... This broken man wants to learn and grow with you by his side. I know it's sudden, I'm more than aware that it's sudden. I don't know how long we have before someone discovers that I am a Kingsman rather than an Inquisitor, and I want to make the most of what time we do have. Will you become my wife, and the mother to my children?"

Anca's lips were curled into a soft smile as she held her finger out. "I would love to marry you."

The ring fit beautifully, and Flick brushed a strand of hair from her face as he rested his forehead against her. "I love you, Anca."

"I love you too, Flick... When will we be wed? As you said, there's little time as far as we know that we are safe."

Flick pulled away just enough to regard her face, silent for a moment. "When do you want to marry me? I can do it as soon as in two days; all I need is to find an officiant, and get you a secondary-"

"I don't need any other ring; this one is beautiful and it's all I need," Anca said quietly "Do we need less time, then?"

He shook his head in response. "No. I want to get our things packed to leave as soon as we can, then. We can get out of Zanther without anyone finding out about us and then we don't need to worry about the repercussions." He cupped Anca's cheek gently. "I want you and the kids to be safe. That's my biggest priority right now."

The smile that flooded Anca's face made his heart melt before he hugged her once more and simply held her close. She leaned into him, and, for a moment, Flick felt like everything would be alright, "We can announce it at the meeting tonight: were you planning on going?"

"I am now," Anca murmured. "I suppose I'll see you there."

It didn't take long before stampeding footsteps rang throughout the house and the two were met by Drop and Shatter. They clung to Flick's legs and then to Anca as Miss Rani, ever vigilant, gasped over the ring that had delicately been placed on Anca's finger.

"I'd like you to begin to pack the children's things, lightly, for us to go," Flick instructed the nanny. "We're planning on moving soon to start our new life together."

"What about your position?"

"I'll find one wherever we settle." The man waved her off slightly. "Don't worry about it. As we will no longer need your services, I will pay you for the remainder of the year and then some."

"Are you sure?" Miss Rani asked.

Flick nodded and then ushered Anca towards the drawing room. There, for the two hours before their meeting, they pulled various documents from drawers and either stored or destroyed them. Flick was careful to destroy the paperwork he would have kept as an Inquisitor; while he'd be questioned about it if they found him, he'd prefer not to be involved again.

He and Anca entered the meeting after cleaning his house and sat down together. The group was small again, seven, now, including them. The priest spoke quietly about the Holy Texts, this time discussing the need for Kingsmen to recognize HaMelech as the ultimate authority of their lives while living a life pure and pleasing -not sinning on purpose- before the group broke to pray.

Anca beamed as the requests reached them. "We've decided to be married."

The congratulations were nearly deafening for the small group and Flick smiled at his fiancée. Anca continued quietly, "We do need prayers, though, as we're planning on moving and will have two young children with us; if all goes well, we shouldn't need to do this in secret but... We are uncertain of other inquisitors or the High Council."

"My father serves as a High Inquisitor," Flick explained. "He's met Anca and, while I don't think he's realized anything, I've a bad feeling about these next few days."

He held Anca's hand gently as the others around them began to pray over them, his head eventually resting on Anca's as he murmured, "HaMelech, protect us... Keep us safe, bless this marriage. Thank you for my beautiful bride, my wonderful children... The family that I never thought I'd have."

It was a quiet dispersal before Flick gently caught the arm of the priest. "Before you go, please... Would you be able to officiate for us? We want to get married as soon as possible, as we know it isn't safe with my former profession to stay in Zanther."

The priest looked between Flick and Anca and then smiled gently. "I can. When?"

"Tomor-"

"Tonight," Anca interrupted quietly, glancing at Flick. "I know you probably want the children there, but with Miss Rani..."

"No, no, doing it without the children is likely the smartest idea. I don't want it to be loud, and Miss Rani cannot know that we're doing this." Flick nodded slightly and took Anca's hand. "Are you alright with it just being us?"

"HaMelech is over us, He knows this union is binding. But... Will I return home with you?" Anca asked quietly. "Miss Rani-"

"Miss Rani won't think anything of it if you stay the night. If you'd really like, we can put you in the guest room until she retires for the evening." Flick brushed a strand of hair from her face. "Do you want to be married tonight?"

Anca stared at him and then nodded. "Tonight."

The priest looked between them. "Alright... It's sudden, are you certain of this?"

"Absolutely."

They held one another's hands and faced each other as the priest began to speak, "This union is a covenant under the eyes of HaMelech; it is a promise to love and cherish one another through sickness, health, times of trouble or joy...." His words faded as Flick stared at Anca, watching her focus on the priest and then him. He smiled lightly at her and she smiled back as the priest murmured, "As long as you both shall live?"

"I do," Flick murmured. "I will love and hold, honor and protect as long as I live."

"And do you, Anca..."

"I do."

"The Holy Text tells us that two are strong, but a cord of three is stronger; keep HaMelech at the head of your marriage and walk towards Him as you build a life on your faith and faithfulness. As HaMelech as your witness, you may now kiss the bride."

Flick gently pulled Anca close and then kissed her, keeping her near as she melted against him. "I swear on my life, Anca, that I will keep you and our children as safe as I possibly can."

Anca brushed some hair from his face and gave him another kiss before she murmured, "We didn't get you a ring..."

"Until we're safe, likely in Blackrock, I don't want to wear one. It's too risky to put one on and show others that I am, in fact, married without a Solari ceremony." Flick kissed her once more and then held her hand. "We can get home, finish packing, and leave tomorrow night. That'll give me enough time to tell my men that I'm leaving while letting us slip away without notice."

He led her from the meeting place after the priest spoke a prayer of protection over them and they hurried home. Drop and Shatter were already sleeping when they arrived, prompting Flick and Anca to carefully pack what they could. Most of the things they set aside were items that they wouldn't be able to get anywhere else: heirlooms, some documents, and a handful of bedding pieces. Anca was certain they could get the couple of items she needed before they left.

Eventually, Flick sunk onto the bed and Anca lowered herself beside him. They didn't speak for several moments before Anca whispered, "What now?"

"Well... We could sleep, or we could just... Lay here together... Or..." Flick trailed off and gave a bit of a shrug. "It's entirely up to you... Mrs. Alastar."

He smiled as Anca's cheeks grew bright red and she murmured, "Ah."

"Don't be frightened, Anca," Flick reassured softly, "I'm not going to hurt you."

"I didn't think you would. I'm just... You must remember that this is the first relationship I've had at all, Flick," Anca admitted softly. "I've no idea what I'm doing."

The cote rested a gentle hand on her own. "Why don't you come lay with your head on my chest, is that alright? Just get used to being beside someone."

She scooted closer to him and closed her eyes as Flick began to rub over her back. "I love you."

"I love you too, Flick," she whispered back.

They rested together for a long while before Flick whispered, "You're going to be a wonderful mother for Drop and Shatter. They love you."

"Hm..." Anca murmured. She glanced up at him. "Would you want another child... With me?"

"Eventually." Flick kissed her softly. "I want to get to know you better first, though." He began to play with her hair and Anca giggled softly. "What? Why are you laughing?'

"I'm just laughing at the fact that here I am, married... Married to a fiercely protective father to two beautiful children. I never expected to get married young, let alone become a mother upon becoming married."

Flick smiled a bit. "Well, surprise."

Anca laughed again and poked him slightly. "Thank you, Flick... I suppose we should rest, shouldn't we?"

"Unless there's something else you'd be comfortable in doing?" Flick asked, cupping her cheek and giving her a kiss. Anca made a little hum in response and Flick smiled against her lips. "I love you."

"I love you too."

CHAPTER NINE

Where Resolve Is Tested

Morning came far too quickly for Flick's liking, especially as he was woken by two children jumping on the bed and wrestling above the covers. Flick pulled the blankets over Anca's sleeping form, kissed her bare shoulder, and then shooshed Drop and Shatter. "Miss Anca is sleeping."

"Daddy, is Miss Anca our mommy now?" Drop asked, pausing in her bouncing to stare at him.

"Yes, my love." Flick smoothed some of the little girl's hair down and laid back against the pillows. "You need to be quiet, though, as she's sleeping."

"Sleeping?" Shatter crawled over the bed to peer down at Anca and then poked her cheek. "It's morning!"

"No, small one." Flick pulled Shatter from Anca. "Let her rest; we had a long night."

He got out of the bed and pulled a robe on. "Come on, you two; Miss Rani will be collecting you to have breakfast. I want you both dressed before then..." He paused and looked back at Anca with a soft smile. "Go on, get your clothes. I hear her down the hall."

The children raced down the hallway and Flick watched them duck into the nursery before he returned to the bedroom. He rejoined Anca on the bed and gently rubbed her shoulder, giving a kiss to her neck every so often, until she murmured, "Must I wake up?"

"I won't make you, though I will need to leave for patrol soon," Flick said quietly in return. He kissed her ear, and she rolled over to look at him.

The sunlight dappling over her made Flick stare in silence, a gentle smile on his face. "You're beautiful."

"Stop..."

"No, I mean it. You really are beautiful." Flick kissed her again and then sighed. "I'll see you for lunch, alright? Same spot?"

Anca nodded a bit and then moved to rest her head on his chest. "That sounds nice..."

"I need to go, Anca," he chuckled and kissed her forehead before he got up. "You should get ready for work, too. Miss Rani has the children; I'd like to get back from work and finish packing tonight."

He got himself dressed and then helped Anca with her corset, kissed her once more, and then led her down the stairs. Miss Rani didn't glance at them as they grabbed food, said 'goodbye' to Drop and Shatter, and then left.

He met Anca for lunch in the middle of the day where he simply stared at his new bride. "Do you want to invite your sister over for dinner tonight and we can tell her we're getting married?"

His wife nodded slightly. "I want to at least tell her 'goodbye' before we leave the city, even if it's brief... I spoke to my colleagues, and they've given me the rest of the day to be home. They wish us the best... Though... I was unable to find Marin."

"We can write to her once we reach Blackrock," Flick murmured. "I'll walk you to the main roads, and then meet you at home for dinner."

They shared a gentle kiss before standing and walking. The city was more solemn than it had been previously. Flick kept Anca close as he looked around, watching as the few people who did dot the streets made their way to buildings and remain inside upon entering. He sent Anca off and then hurried to the guard's quarters. "Jordon, what's going on?"

"High Inquisitor Treatis is dead," Jordon said quietly. "The city is in mourning for him while the Council finds his replacement."

Flick swallowed and nodded slowly. "I see. The patrols are running, still, and I know that we must focus on our duties until we receive word otherwise."

"That's another thing. You received another letter."

The other man held out a black envelope with a golden seal. Flick took it silently, willed himself to open it, and took in the words.

It was a summons to the citadel, signed personally by High Inquisitor Gravis. Flick donned his heavy armor with nothing more than a pit of absolute dread in his stomach.

He slowly made his way through the city and entered the Judgement Room. In any other case, the room would be shrouded in shadows. Today, though, as the High Inquisitors were gathered, the room was lit brilliantly. On the wall were blazing swords, each covered in flames from hilt to blade, that served as lanterns. When Flick was younger, he remembered coming with his father and witnessing one of the inquisitors reach his hand through the flames to lift the blade from its set. Unfortunately, the flames burned even through his gloves and the shock killed him soon after.

Sitting around the edge of the round space were 8 thrones. Seven of the thrones had occupants, three women and four men, while the eighth sat empty. A black shroud was placed over the brilliant gold in a silent marking of Treatis' death while they waited to fill the position.

As was customary, Flick entered the room and got onto one knee before the Council. "May Solaris' grace shine bright upon you."

The words made Flick's stomach turn and he kept his eyes downcast to avoid betraying the nausea he felt.

"You may rise."

Flick lifted his head to stare at the seven before him. They all had keen interest in their eyes as they stared him down, though Flick's gaze was fixed on his father. There wasn't much on the older man's face, but Flick could see that there was some semblance of pride.

He had pulled strings, hadn't he?

"Flick Alastar, the Council lost a member overnight," one of the women said lightly. "We were advised to investigate your deeds for Solaris and to evaluate your works regarding this highly sought position.

"We have decided to move favorably with inducting you into the Council of High Inquisitors as to further your duties and faithfulness to Solaris, our Burning Light and the Fire of Justice." She was silent for a moment. "High Inquisitor Alastar will be aiding you in the Rite of Ascension, in which you are prepared to take on your duties as Solaris' arm and weapon."

This wasn't good.

Flick remained on one knee as his father stood and moved towards him. "Thank you for this honor... But... Forgive me, High Inquisitor Lillian, as this is so sudden. I had assumed I would receive more notice before this... That I would be able to be more presentable in the eyes of Solaris."

He fell silent as High Inquisitor Gravis lifted his hand. "That is enough, Alastar... Don't be so modest. Of the inquisitors here in Zanther, you are the most qualified of the candidates. We are very impressed with you and your deeds; you have high favor in Solaris' eyes."

Flick swallowed hard and lowered his head. "HaMelech... Please, get Anca and the kids from Zanther. Help her to know she needs to go... And please, if it's your will, protect me, too..."

Renounce Solaris.

The voice was firm in the back of his mind and Flick swallowed as his father got closer, "Alastar? What are you waiting for? Don your Shroud."

Renounce Solaris, Flick.

Flick gritted his teeth and then looked up. "I will not take this position. Solaris is no deity, nor is he a savior. HaMelech is the True King and it is He that I serve; He is the only God who I will serve and is the only God that I will recognize as sovereign in this world or any other."

Everything went silent as Flick stood there, suddenly aware that the nerves he had felt earlier had been replaced by a feeling of power and a sense of calm. In fact, as he stood at full height, he realized he wasn't afraid of the fate to come.

He stared his father in the eyes, watching as the rage and confusion morphed into a single grimace before he spat, "I have no son."

The rest of the Council drew their swords and the blades ignited; Flick could feel the heat from the weapons even when they were halfway across the room.

His father gave a single swing of his blade and Flick, though he was certain he was going to be slain, managed to avoid the deadly metal. He turned and ran, his eyes darting around as he attempted to find a diversion, before they landed on one of the swords on the wall.

It would sear through his flesh and bone, and there was a high chance that he'd die from shock, but it was still a chance to create a distraction. Flick swerved from where he had been running and lunged for the sword without another thought.

Though it was hot, the fire that wreathed around Flick's hand didn't burn. It felt like a rush of cool water as it licked up his arm and shoulder, brushing against his face for the moment that he held onto the sword to pull it from where it rested, and then flung it towards the drapery and wooden decoration of the Judgement Room.

In an instant, the flames lapped hungrily at the fuel and began to consume everything in their way. Flick ignored his father and the other High Inquisitors as he managed to get to a second and then third sword before he flew through the Grand Doors and slammed them behind him.

On either side of the doorway, the guards looked at Flick and raised their eyebrows.

He merely nodded at them. "Carry on. The High Council is debating, and I thought it best not remain with their tempers so... Firey."

Both guards nodded at him, and he hurried from the entry and towards the final set of doors. As soon as he was under the light of the sun, the citadel bells began to toll an alarm.

Flick dared to glance back in time to see billows of smoke had begun to rise from the citadel's tower and guards were racing towards him. As best he could, he lowered his face and hurried through the crowd as though a bystander. It worked no more than a handful of minutes before he heard someone cry out for him to halt, prompting Flick to break into a sprint.

It was as though each guard knew they were after him the moment he was spotted; Flick took a turn down one road to see there were men coming towards him, and then he would turn and go a different way only to see someone else cornering him there. He had nearly given up when a door halfway down an alley opened and the occupant waved to him. "Over here!"

The cote didn't attempt to recognize the man as he slid to a halt and then turned to run towards him, ever aware of footsteps running after him. He dove into the stranger's home and hit the ground, turning in time to see the familiar face of Osmond, who had threatened him weeks earlier, before he blinked, and he was lying on the floor of his study.

Anca was in the other room, laughing as she played with Drop and Shatter. He forced himself to move from where he lay, "Anca! Anca!"

His abrupt calls silenced the playing and Anca hurried to his side. He gripped her arms and searched her face. "I need you to take the children and run."

"What?"

"They know. The High Inquisitors know. I denounced Solaris in front of them, they were going to make me ascend. I told them that Solaris was not a god and that HaMelech is the only King I will serve."

Anca's face drained of color, and she swayed slightly before Flick lowered her to the ground. "We need to go, right now. We have maybe a half-hour before the entire city will be looking for me. I need you to get the children to Garren's Stand and I want you to wait no more than 3 days for me to follow. Get to Blackrock. I know there's a Kingsman quarter there that can protect the three of you."

"You need to come with us, Flick, I can't leave you behind. We just... We just got married." Anca blinked up at him. "Please, don't make me leave you-"

"I love you, that's why I need to stay back... At least until you can escape." Flick pulled her into a tight hug and pressed his nose in her hair, "It'll be alright, HaMelech will protect us."

He ran into his study in order to get a decent sized pouch of gems, a pack for Anca to keep a couple of rations, a blanket to keep the children warm, and then his mantle. He carefully put the feathered shawl into the pack with the gems, gathered his children, and then glanced out the window to the street.

He could see a merchant just down the block, the man lazily picking at his teeth as he watched city guard run from alley to alley.

As soon as Flick caught sight of an opening, he ushered his family outside. "Are you leaving Zanther proper?"

"Yes, sir. Why-"

"5 gold, no questions asked, you take these three to Garren's Stand," Flick interrupted. "There's a handful of belongings but move-out day has come, and they haven't transportation yet."

The driver raised an eyebrow. "5 gold?"

"Ten if you keep your mouth shut and just agree."

"It's a deal. 10 gold to transport the miss and the children." The driver gestured to the back of his wagon and Flick carefully placed his children into it.

Anca climbed in without help but turned to face Flick. "Please, be careful."

"I will. And you two, I need you to play a game with your mother; whoever speaks or makes a sound loses. Alright?"

Wide eyed nods answered him, and Flick pulled blankets around them. "I love you all."

"I love you too, Flick." Anca stared at him once more before she embraced him. "HaMelech protect you."

A sense of peace washed over him, and he pulled away to regard his family. "I'll see you in Garren's Stand."

Before he knew it, the wagon had lurched away and was gone.

Flick stared after it for a moment before he hurried back to his house.

At any minute, Inquisitors would be at his door. His father would likely be leading them as he was embarrassed by Flick's action- how could he not be when Flick publicly declared that Solaris was false? - and Flick had no doubt that the moment he entered the street he would be subject to death or capture.

He stood beside a window to watch as the streets burst with activity; guards, Inquisitors, and high Inquisitors all milled around as they looked for him. As he expected, an inquisitor with a patrol was rapidly approaching.

The cote made his way deeper into the house. If they were going to look for him here, he might as well force them to really look.

It wasn't until he was properly hidden, his blade sheathed at his side and his armor on, that Flick stopped moving. He sat in silence for what felt like hours before he heard footsteps enter. "He's in here. Search the area!"

Trust me.

Flick stiffened at the voice and then sighed. This was going to kill him, he had to stay hidden-

Trust me, Flick.

With another heavy sigh, Flick slowly moved from his hiding place and lifted his hands. "I surrender."

The group of guards and inquisitors stopped and looked towards Flick almost dumbly.

It took several minutes before someone finally grabbed Flick's arms and forced his hands behind him. His sword was removed and, while not enough to bruise him, he was forced from his home. Briefly, he glanced back to see that what belongings he had left were being cast into the fire, but as far as he knew they weren't attempting to find his children.

Any relief he felt was short lived as Flick realized that he was not being led to the primary dungeon below the citadel but, instead, to a keep belonging to one of the High Inquisitors. The Alastar family coat of arms, two ravens with arrows thrust through their necks, proudly adorned the large oak door and, without any doubt, hid his father inside.

High Inquisitor Fernando Alastar was waiting as the guards pulled Flick inside, and he took his son by the hair to drag him into one of the torture chambers. There, he manacled Flick to a stone table. "Repent, Flick."

"HaMelech is good-" Flick cried out as his father simply laid the glowing hot metal of his sword against Flick's chest. It melted through his linen shirt and seared his skin, wounding it as Fernando lifted the blade.

"Who is the High God!"

"My King is HaMelech!"

Again, the red-hot metal seared Flick and he cried out again.

This happened over, and over again before a knock sounded. Flick took the brief interruption as a chance to breathe as a guard entered and saluted. "Sir, we captured all four you had us look for."

"Excellent, bring them in."

As Flick turned his head to see what was happening, his gaze first met the familiar blue eyes of Adriata and then of Anca before he realized that they, and his children, were manacled together at the wrists. In an instant, Fernando donned the Shroud of Solaris and turned towards them: Adriata squeaked in fright and flinched.

With his attention now on her, Fernando leaned in. "Who is the Most High God?"

"S-Solaris! Solaris the Radiant!" Adriata whispered, "Solaris is the Most High God!"

Fernando stared at her for a moment before he straightened. "Excellent... This one will be free to go." He then turned to Anca. "Who is the Most-"

"I serve the True King HaMelech, and no other," Anca interrupted, lifting her chin as she stared at him.

Adriata's little gasp did nothing but aid the chaos as Fernando drove the pommel of his blade into Anca's face. A spray of blood covered his otherwise pristine armor as he broke her nose and made the children scream, but Anca, aside from staggering ever so slightly, righted herself.

"You picked a woman with backbone, I will give you that…" Fernando turned back towards Flick. "Deceiving, manipulating, and of filthy blood… But stupidly brave." He offered a chuckle, wiping the blood from the pommel of his sword. "If you wanted in her pants, Flick, you didn't have to go through the effort of pretending to be a heretic… Release the first one's chains and lead her from here. As for the other blonde and the children, place them in a cell."

As the guards nodded and did as he asked, Fernando leaned over Flick. The heat of his blade licked Flick's face and caused it to burn, forcing the stone that it rested on to begin to bubble. "I was considering sending your concubine to burn tomorrow, but I decided that there is something worse. You and your tainted offspring are going to rot in my dungeon. Each day, you will grow hungrier and hungrier, and each day I will personally make your life a living hell for disrespecting *my* family name. Each evening, you will be thrown into a dark cell where you can see and hear your children starving to death, but you will be unable to comfort them. As for your woman," Fernando grinned, "I may even have a guard rape her in front of you each day. You will be helpless, broken, and bruised… But don't worry, you will not be alone. I've arranged for you to have a cellmate: your heretical witches are predicable if nothing else, and this one will keep you alive so that I can continue to break you." He paused for a moment, staring down at his son as Flick tried to move from the heat of his sword. "That is… Unless you repent, then all of this can end."

Flick swallowed, staring at his father, before he shut his eyes. "HaMelech will not abandon me, regardless of what you do."

"Very well."

Screams echoed through the private dungeon as Fernando burned, bruised, and broke Flick. Eventually, Flick was thrown into a small cell.

He lay in a pile, able to hear Anca and his children in a cell across from him.

Drop and Shatter were sobbing as Anca tried desperately to soothe them, and Flick groaned as he forced himself to stand. "Are you alright? Did they touch you?"

"No... No, we are okay. One tried to touch me, but I slapped his hand away and he didn't try again," Anca reassured amid the sobbing. "Are you okay? Flick, what is he going to do to us?"

Flick was silent for a moment, finally opening his mouth to explain when the door clicked open again. Hurriedly, he struggled to the bars nearest his family. "I'm sorry this happened, all of it... They're going to starve you and break me. I'm so sorry, Anca, I cannot do anything for you or the children and... HaMelech help us, I cannot do anything...."

Footsteps echoed down the stone path before a woman with wavy red hair, followed by a guard, appeared. She was forced into Flick's cell where she remained still for a moment and then sat up as soon as the guard left. "Praise HaMelech..."

"You were down below," Flick whispered. "Is that where they brought you from?"

She glanced at him, her eyes wide as she nodded, and then she reached out. "Hold still, you're absolutely battered..."

"Please, leave it. It'll do nothing but cause more trouble in the long run..."

"I must do something... My name is Marin, just sit still and-"

"Marin?"

"Anca?"

The two women hurried to the edge of their cells, outstretching their hands as though they could clasp one another's, before Marin hurriedly explained that she had been sentenced to death on the pyre when she was pulled from her cell and brought here. Anca, as Flick laid down again and closed his eyes to regain his strength, explained what happened to them and they then fell silent.

Eventually, Marin moved to Flick's side. "Flick, please, let me tend to your wounds."

"He will open them again," Flick murmured.

"Please."

As soon as Flick relented, the woman rested her hands on his arms and began to pray. A soft, golden sheen raised over his wounds and began to seal each cut shut. Flick didn't mind it, really, aside from knowing what would happen the day after.

Just as he assumed, each day his father entered the cell, asked if he had thought about anything, and then proceeded to beat him into a bloody pulp. Marin healed him again, and then again, before Fernando would return.

There was no sense of time as this happened, and each day grew progressively more painful as Drop and Shatter's cries for food and their father echoed through the cells. Flick and Marin attempted to toss some of their food to the kids, but not much was able to happen as guards remained until they had eaten their fill and then took the remainder away.

Flick watched as Anca did her best to keep their spirits up, washing their hair at one point and then their faces before she finally sat down and simply held the children. "Flick…"

"Yes, my love? Are they both still alive? Are you alive?" Flick whispered. He had taken to simply laying there as he waited for death to come or for the magots attracted to his wounds, but this time he forced himself to stand and slowly move to the front-most portion of his cell.

His wife's thin, pale arm reached out towards him to grasp his hand but, as it always was, they were unable to reach. Anca's arm withdrew, and her quiet, trembling voice murmured, "I don't know how much longer they can do this. Neither of them are remaining awake for more than a few hours at a time now, and I can tell that I... I'm exhausted, too."

"I... I know. I'll do what I can to get them something to eat today; maybe Marin can distract the guards or... Or..." Flick trailed off, the sense of failure and guilt falling over him heavier than he had expected. He sunk to the ground, rested one hand on the bar, and closed his eyes. "If I renounce HaMelech, this will stop."

"No, it won't: you know it won't. You'll renounce HaMelech and he kills us, and then you die a horrible death and face judgement where you must justify yourself to the King," Anca whispered. "Please, Flick... It will be okay. If... If we don't make it, then at least we will see each other in HaMelech's arms."

"*I* am the reason our children are dying. I'm the reason that guards come in here and look at you like you're nothing more than a piece of meat. Anca, I'm the reason that we have no future out of this cell.... And.... And I am so sorry that I caused this. If I had told you the truth of who I was, we could have left sooner..."

A femur clattered against his cell, and he opened his eyes to see that Anca, her hair wildly unkempt and her face sunken, was standing. She had another bone at the ready to throw at him. "Don't you dare blame yourself for anything your father has done! You are nothing like that monster, and you never will be. It is his hardened heart that has kept us here, and while it hasn't proven us dead yet, our blood will be on his hands should we die. It is *not* your fault; do you hear me?"

Flick scoffed quietly. "Sure, Anca..." he paused, ignoring his wife as she began to argue with him, and tilted his head. He was sure he heard something.... "Sh."

This time, what looked like a rib bone tumbled through the air and hit Flick in the chest. He glared at Anca, meeting her angry blue eyes. "Don't shush me, Flick Alastar. I have every right-"

"I hear something, Anca. Stop talking for just a moment, please," he snapped back.

His wife stopped, blinked at him, and then tilted her head to listen as well.

Quiet metal on metal scratched through the air, not like sword on sword but like a key in a lock. Flick frowned before he glanced towards the door. "Someone is breaking in."

"What do you mean 'someone is breaking in'?" Marin whispered, "Who's crazy enough to try getting into a High Inquisitor's keep?"

Flick shook his head before he gritted his teeth and sunk down. Some of the constant pain in his ribs had flared up, but as Marin approached, he waved her back. "No... I cannot do it anymore, Marin. Please, just let me hurt and let me succumb to it."

About that time, Anca's quiet voice caught his attention. "Drop, Drop, look at me... Keep your eyes open and look at me..."

It went silent as a latch caught and the sound of the door to the keep opening filled the air.

All eyes in the cells flashed to the now open entrance, breaths bated, before two figures slunk in and shut the door behind them. One of them was taller than the other and wore a heavy trench coat and an adventuring backpack. It took him only a moment to shrug off the jacket and pack to reveal that there was yet another backpack on his shoulders, this one with a rams' head. Flick recognized this as a RAMS suit, something that he had only heard about as Kingsmen wore them. The man beside him was a cote with sharp falcon eyes and a hooked beak. He was wearing lighter, leather armor and had stashed a bow on his back as he followed the taller man inside.

"Olare? Olare, Rolandus, over here!" Marin whispered, moving to the front of the cell and waving one of her arms. "I can't believe you're here... What are you doing?"

"Getting you out of here," Olare, the man in the suit, said. "What do you think you're doing, making a High Inquisitor so mad-"

"I don't know why he brought me here aside for the purposes of torturing this man." Marin gestured to Flick, and the raven cote offered a weak smile. "We need to get out. There are two children and their mother in the cell across from us and they haven't eaten for however long we've been trapped here-"

"From what we were told, in knowing you were captured 2 weeks ago..." Rolandus, the falcon, trailed off before he hurried to Anca's cell. Flick was unable to see his family past the other man, but as he muttered a couple of curses under his breath, Flick could only assume the worst.

It took several minutes before a little 'click' filled the air and Rolandus swung the cell door open. "Olare, help them out; the children seem completely faded... Marin, I hope you're able to focus..."

"I've been praying over them. They're starving; they haven't eaten in two weeks, they need food, or they aren't going to make it," Anca said.

Flick's sight was blocked again as Olare stepped into his view, leaving him nothing but worry as he listened to Anca and the man speak in hushed tones as Rolandus began to pick the lock to his cell. As soon as the door was open, Flick attempted to stand to get to his family but collapsed. Marin hesitated, briefly, and he shook his head. "Help them first. I'll be okay."

He remained where he was until Rolandus came to him and carefully pulled him up. "Who are you to have gotten into this mess, Friend?"

Despite the worry Flick had for his family, he allowed himself to stand and murmur, "The son of a High Inquisitor... Who renounced Solaris in front of him." He didn't say anything else, instead attempting to crane his head. "Are they okay? Anca, are the children okay?"

"Just a moment, my love... They look awful, but Olare has some dried rations..."

Her words earned a sigh of relief and Flick hung his head, nearly losing his balance, as Rolandus helped him from the cell. "Son of a High Inquisitor, a traitor to Zanther... This is a new story, Friend. What's your name?"

"Flick... Flick Alastar. The women and children are my family; they are Anca, Drop, and Shatter."

"Flick Alastar..." Rolandus mused. He held Flick up in order to get him to a good place to sit. "Rest here, let me help get your children and wife from their cell..."

In just a few short minutes, Flick had his arms wrapped around the gaunt forms of his children and had Anca on his other side. He clung to them, each, despite the pain it caused him as they cried. Neither child understood why they kept witnessing their grandfather beat Flick, and neither of them understood why they weren't being fed; there was so much done to them in these acts that Flick felt nothing more than heartbreak and agony for the children he had worked so hard to protect.

Anca sobbed into Flick's shoulder and he pressed her head into his chest. "I have you, it's okay... It's going to be okay..."

Rolandus, Olare, and Marin stood over them silently before Rolandus murmured, "We need to get you out of here. Let them calm down, as we cannot risk them making noise-"

"The tunnels will not echo," Flick said quietly. "They're soundproof until you get near an exit, and even then..."

The three Kingsmen above them glanced at one another and Olare raised an eyebrow. "Tunnels?"

Flick attempted to stand and stumbled into Rolandus' arms. The other cote helped him steady himself, allowing Olare to lift Drop and Shatter while Marin helped Anca, before Flick limped towards the two pillars in the far corner. He could hear Marin quietly encouraging Anca to take another step, but to be gentle on herself as she hadn't eaten in so long, while Olare shushed a whimper that rose from Shatter.

Setting his jaw, Flick ran a hand over the stone before he felt the small, palm-sized indent that marked these hidden doors. He pressed firmly into that spot to push it when Rolandus, seeing what he was doing, joined.

A door slowly opened as they pushed and, breathing heavily, Flick stood back. "There... In, quickly... He has... He has yet to come by today."

Olare ushered Marin and Anca into the tunnel first and then followed them. Rolandus raised an eyebrow at Flick. "The son of an inquisitor wouldn't be told this."

"No... But a potential High Inquisitor would have been," Flick murmured. He stepped inside with Rolandus' help and pushed the door closed, slowly moving through the group in order to take the lead beside the other cote. "Stay close, do not stray. These tunnels are meant to be the death of those who do not know them... What side of the city do we need to be on?"

"Through the sewer district," Olare said, from behind him.

Flick nodded faintly, limping along. Every so often he'd have the group stop and he'd run his hand on the wall, and then the other wall, before he'd take a turn. Finally, Rolandus asked, "What are you looking for?"

"Inquisitors spend their entire first three years training to be able to read the symbols on the walls. They're nothing more than different palm shapes in different directions, which are unnoticeable otherwise," Flick explained quietly. They were able to get a good distance through the tunnels before he had to sit, breathing heavily through gritted teeth.

Anca crouched in front of him, "Are you going to be okay?"

"I... Think so. Just let me have a moment to breathe." Flick pressed his forehead to hers, doing his best not to betray the agony flaring through his ribs, "What a horrible honeymoon..."

"You're newlywed?" Olare asked, glancing at Marin, "I thought these children were yours."

"They are, through marriage," Anca replied quietly, "Flick is their father, and I am their mother."

"Anca does not have children of her own, Olare, but Flick did." Marin rested a hand on Drop's back and a soft, golden light shone through her hand as she murmured, "They told me that they were wed the day before their capture."

"We have had a single night together, and the rest were here in this cell," Flick said bitterly. "If I hadn't been so careless in what I was doing-"

"It wasn't your fault. They found us as they knew what they were looking for." Anca rested a hand on his cheek and Flick leaned into it with a sigh. He nodded, quietly, before Anca helped him stand and they leaned into one another.

They were unable to take more than a step together before Marin and Rolandus caught them and helped them each walk. After that point, the group was silent. Flick found the various paths they needed to take in order to get out, though he did pause. "What day and time is it?"

Rolandus raised an eyebrow "We managed to get to you... It was just before noon, and today is the 18th-"

"Perfect. Change of plan; take the next left and then the next right," Flick said, struggling beside Rolandus. "We don't have much time, since people will be coming back by 2:00-"

"How do you know we have enough time?" Olare asked, shifting Shatter and Drop. "People don't just-"

"They do when the guard patrol hasn't changed in four months, and the inquisitor in charge of this specific barracks never liked to change

the patrol... Meaning his partner would have been the last one to do so."
Flick offered a weak smirk before they arrived at a long tunnel with a
ladder running towards what looked like a wooden hatch in the ceiling.

Olare was the first up, leaving Drop and Shatter with the others,
before he poked his head down. "Pass up the children; the barracks are
completely empty, and from what I can tell, the streets-"

"You're going to want to go through the back door; Jordon uses it
to smoke, but every patrol comes in from the front," Flick interrupted
quietly. "It'll lead into an alley that we can then navigate."

Rolandus and Olare spared one another a glance and Anca, as she
caught her breath, shook her head. "You can trust him; Flick is a good
man, and he would never do something that would risk his children."

"And if he is wrong?"

"Then I hope they are quicker at killing Kingsmen than my father is,"
Flick said dryly.

It took a moment for them to pass through the guardhouse as Olare
and Rolandus pulled the trench coat over the taller man and attached
the 'adventuring pack' onto it. Flick had to admit that the disguise was
genius, as no one would question something like this in the city.

Just as he had said, the passage through the guardhouse was clear
and they made it into the alley without any difficulties. It was when
they began to make their way through the alley, towards the street, and
a lone figure entered the alley with a smoking pipe in his mouth that
Flick ushered the group back, "Go, go, now-"

"You know, it was very rude of you to just... Disappear, Flick. You
left me with filling your patrols, and that's left me precious little time
to visit Adriata and her girls," the figure said. Flick grimaced as he
recognized the voice was indeed Jordon, and his blood ran cold as the
other man continued. "Why didn't you share that you had children?
Didn't you trust me after all we'd been through?"

"Jordon, it really doesn't need to be this way," Flick said quietly. "No one needs to know-"

"Of course, that's a lie. Your father would appreciate knowing that his prisoners have escaped, and I'm certain that the other High Inquisitors would like to know this as well, too." Jordon stopped within a dozen paces and drew his blade to let it hang casually by his side, "It's a pity, though. You would have made a wonderful High Inquisitor if this bitch didn't get in your head."

"That's my wife, Jordon," Flick finally hissed, struggling faintly to stand away from Rolandus. "I swear, if you hurt her-"

"Blah, blah, blah... This will only hurt a little." Jordon grinned as flames ignited along the blade of his weapon, "I'm going to enjoy this."

Olare stepped in front of the group, his hardlight blade beginning to glow in his hands, "Just stay back. Let me handle him until you have an opening to run."

"Let us at least cover your back," Rolandus said. Now that Flick was mostly upright, Rolandus drew his stringless bow. From the tip hung a single falcon feather tied on with straps of leather: Flick had no doubt that this was a second mantle in case his first was ruined.

Jordon snicked at them and muttered something under his breath. Flick could hardly remember what it was he had said, but as the air around him began to shimmer and distort as though from a great heat, it shot into memory; it was another blessing of Solaris. "Olare, be careful... Solaris has imbued him with more power..."

"Well done, Flick: you did pay attention in school." Jordon chuckled before he flew at Olare. Their weapons clashed with a shower of hot sparks, the intensity of the flashes growing as Jordon brought his blade against Olare's time and time again with relentless force.

Rolandus backed the group up as best he could, holding his bow as though at the ready while waiting for Olare to move from his shot. It was only when Olare managed to lock Jordon's blade with his own that

Jordon was forced into a bind: Olare's RAM suit ensured that he held the strength advantage by a wide margin.

Rather than using this to slay Jordon, Olare forced his bodyweight forward in order to throw Jordon down. The inquisitor rolled backwards onto his feet while Olare pushed the group backwards again and Rolandus, with distance now made, pulled back on a delicate golden strand that suddenly appeared on his bow.

A salvo of brilliant glowing projectiles flew towards Jordon but, with Solaris' protection, were redirected into near misses.

Jordon wiped a bit of grime from his face, grinning and squaring up again. "Having friends fight for you... I'll have to keep that in mind for next time."

He dove at Olare once more, prodding and darting at the Kingman until Olare locked blades once more.

This time, Jordon was ready; he rolled into it, pulling a blade from his side. The metal burst into flames and Jordon, without hesitation, plunged it into Olare's arm just below the shoulder.

Flick watched as Olare staggered back, his arm useless as the metal seared through it, and instead did his best to block any incoming blows with his off hand.

There had to be something that he could do to help.

Flick's eyes darted around to find a weapon he could use before he realized that Anca had darted forward with her hands outstretched. Just like she had done at the Long Night, a golden dome formed above herself and Olare. Jordon swung at it, repeatedly, but did nothing aside from send sparks up as the Dove gave Olare a moment to breathe.

It wasn't going to last long, though, as Jordon used his full bodyweight to beat into the shield. Anca's arms were trembling even after a few moments, which made Flick's desperate search lower his definition of weapon from 'blade' to 'anything'. He caught sight of a wooden staff with an iron band around one end beside a small pile of rubbish, filling his definition, and without a second thought he grabbed it. Marin had his children, Rolandus would be able to grab Anca and Olare... He'd have to stay back to try and subdue Jordon but it was at least better than them all dying.

With that in mind, a burst of adrenaline filled Flick, helping him to forget the pain that had spread through his body, and he ran. The shield was a solid footing as he hit it, using it to get up and above Jordon, before he jumped and brought the improvised weapon down.

Jordon stumbled back to meet it with his blade, producing sparks and flames that licked up around the wood that Flick wielded. Rather than the staff being burned, it held Jordon's blade back before Flick pulled away and then brought the staff down once more.

This time, as the staff caught Jordon's blade, Flick was met with the reminder of how many years he had spent training alongside his friend. Each blow was blocked as he did his best to force Jordon back before Jordon kicked one of his legs out.

Flick hit the cobblestone and Jordon's blade came down in time for a golden blade to manifest from the staff and over his chest. No longer was it a staff but a scythe, and as Flick kept Jordon from ending him, he whispered, "Jordon, please... I forgive you; you can come with us, know HaMelech, and have a new life-"

"I will never follow a false king, and I'd never bend to follow the worm you follow, Alastar," Jordon hissed.

He raised his sword, ignoring the arrows that Rolandus fired, before Flick lunged with his scythe. The weapon caught Jordon with the blunt edge, forcing him off balance, and then Flick swung a single time. With a scream, it sliced through Jordon and forced him to his knees as blood began to pool around him.

All Flick could do was stare at his friend, tears beginning to streak down his face as Jordon clung to his wounded side and then coughed, "I *hate* you..."

"Jordon..."

"Guards!" Jordon's voice was thin through the alley as it echoed and Flick, who stared at him, only broke line of sight as Rolandus grabbed his shoulder.

"We don't have time. Your friend... It is HaMelech's grace that determines his fate. We need to go," the falcon cote said quietly. "You did all you could."

Flick offered a silent nod before he turned away from Jordon and the small group began to run through the alley once more.

CHAPTER TEN

Where Hope Begins

I t didn't take long before they found a small section of wall hidden behind brush and rubbish that proved to be a hole that they could leave through, one that led them directly out of the walls and to two gigantic rams. The beasts lifted their heads lazily to regard them, shifted upon Marin placing Drop and Shatter atop one of them, and then bleated as Rolandus and Flick got to Olare.

His arm was still useless and smelled of nothing but burnt flesh. Flick could easily see that the burn was a third-degree one at best and that any nerves within were cauterized. Olare grimaced as he attempted to flex his hand but couldn't move it. Marin rested a hand on his arm, "We'll have to remove the arm, Olare-"

"Don't you dare touch it, Marin," Olare said quietly, "It'll be okay."

"You're not a sea star, Olare, so it won't grow back," Marin said quietly, "Get onto the ram, I can't do anything here. We'll look at it closer when we get to the hold-"

"The hold?" Flick asked quietly. He held himself up on the scythe, which now was a staff again, "How far is it?"

"Two days' ride, if we stop," Rolandus said. He glanced at the other ram, studying Anca and the children, "We'll have to stop at least once for them to have something to eat, but it's a swift ride otherwise."

Flick nodded slowly and moved to the ram where Anca held Drop and Shatter. He gently rested his hand on each of their heads, offering a small smile, "We will be somewhere safe soon... Will you be alright to ride?"

"We haven't a choice, do we?" Anca asked quietly. She offered a small smile, "We'll be okay; I've no doubt that we will travel as a group and be able to rest once we arrive wherever it is that we're going."

They shared a gentle kiss before Rolandus and Marin came over, "Olare says he can ride with one hand; you'll be riding with him and Marin if you trust me with your wife and children."

Flick nodded again at Rolandus before he was helped onto the ram, and they took off through the forest.

It took a little bit before he dared to speak over the racing wind, "How did you find us?"

"We were looking for Marin!" Olare called back, "Word came that she was captured, and we were trying to find her. HaMelech was good in placing you with her; we wouldn't have found you otherwise!"

The ride continued until Flick's eyes grew too heavy to remain open. He slumped against Olare's back, just able to hear Marin's worried voice carrying over the wind as she asked the man to stop.

When he next opened his eyes, they were resting beside a rocky outcrop. Anca had the children wrapped in a blanket each as they drank what looked like a thin broth and Marin, beside Olare, was wrapping his arm with a clean bandage. As soon as they realized he was awake, Marin murmured, "How do you feel?"

"Like I can't breathe," Flick said, turning over to cough violently.

"It's your ribs again, isn't it?" Anca asked quietly, "This was like when he beat you..."

Flick glanced at his wife and offered a weak smile, "I'm sure it's nothing more than residual."

"I want to check them as soon as we're at the hold. Until then, drink some of this; it's a mixture of herbs that will help with the pain." Marin scooted over to him and rested her hands on his side. Flick was unable to keep from flinching, having come to expect this following more severe pain. Marin shut her eyes and began to pray over him, making him sigh as the feeling of cool water washed over him, "That will help until we're back."

"Thank you... I guess we never formally met either of your friends, Marin," Flick said quietly, "We know their names, but..."

"I'm Olare Culbert, Marin's half-brother," the older man murmured, "and Rolandus is my friend and confidant."

Flick looked at the falcon cote to see that he had removed his mantle to reveal a man no older than twenty. He was polishing his bow quietly, though he did offer a nod before Flick spoke, "I'm Flick... And this is my wife Anca and our children, Drop and Shatter."

"You said you were just married?" Rolandus asked.

Anca spoke up from where she was, prompting Flick to slowly move to her side and take Shatter into his arms, "The night before they found us. Flick and I were wed in a Kingsman ceremony and the next morning he was summoned to the citadel. We tried to escape through the north gate, but the moment they were on the hunt for Flick, they were looking for us. They found the children and I, as well as my sister... Oh, Flick, Adriata..."

Flick wrapped his arm around Anca as she began to cry, leaving him to murmur, "Adriata proclaimed Solaris, and found out at that time that Anca follows HaMelech. That's the last we saw of her, prior to my father taking us further into chains."

"Well... Congratulations on the marriage, and I'm sorry that married life has been this hectic," Rolandus said quietly. He watched the little family for a moment before he turned back to his bow, "All of you should get some sleep; it's easier to rest now than it will be on the back of a ram... Unless you're like Flick, from what I was told."

A soft laugh rang through the little group before Flick shifted, "Before we rest... What happened with the staff?"

"It seems you've been picked by a relic weapon, though I've yet to run into writings about a scythe," Olare said, holding his good arm out. Flick passed him the staff carefully and Olare inspected it, "What all do they teach you about hard-light weapons as an Inquisitor?"

Flick watched the older man, "Not much; we know that only Kingsmen can wield them, but that's about it."

"Not Kingsmen in general, but Knights of the Long Road... Well, more or less. They're the warriors who are either chosen by HaMelech or who give their life to HaMelech to serve. Rolandus and I are both Knights, while Marin and... Remind me your name, Mrs....?"

"Anca Alastar," Anca said quietly.

"Right. Marin and your wife, Anca, are Doves. They are called by HaMelech to heal or who choose to do so for HaMelech. As for this scythe, it appears that HaMelech is calling you into service." Olare held the staff out to Flick, prompting Flick to go over it as Olare continued, "Hard-light weapons are blessed by His hand and appear when they are needed. Some are passed through generations, but relics like this- and Rolandus' bow- are buried with their user until HaMelech calls them into service again. They're to be used only to further HaMelech's message and to protect those who are susceptible to the lies of the enemy."

"Like... when I used it against Jordon?"

Olare nodded, "If it were being used selfishly, or without wisdom, I have no doubt in my mind that it would have vanished from your hand the moment you swung. Until you misuse it, or you pass into HaMelech's arms, this is yours."

Flick offered a smile before realizing how exhausted he was. He moved, slowly, to Anca and the kids. There, he curled up with his wife and pulled their children close for a fitful rest beside the fire.

They were roused and placed onto the rams again soon after they fell asleep. Flick's back and seat were sore as they continued to ride, finally picking their way through the mountains and to a relatively well-hidden cave. There, Flick was surprised to see a camp of nearly 20 Kingsmen and Doves who, upon their arrival, were quick to help them down and get them settled. Drop and Shatter were instantly wrapped in blankets and a Dove tended to each while a third Dove gently checked Anca over. Marin helped Flick and Olare to a quieter section of the cave where she had Flick remove his shirt in order to inspect his ribs and Olare do the same for his arm.

Flick could see the swelling hadn't gone down and the wounds that had remained open were festering with maggots. Marin gagged, "At least it's clean.... They did well in that..."

Without another word, she set upon cleaning each of his wounds with stinging soap and hot water before she had a second Dove join her. Together, they began to stitch various wounds, shift bones back to where they needed to go, and prayed over Flick's battered body so that he might be healed.

Then, they turned to Olare.

"Alright, you can either try and fall asleep or we can give you a strap of leather to bite," Marin said quietly, "We don't have anything to put you under, but with the knife having been so hot, it's a matter of cutting through already deadened flesh."

"Marin, I'll be okay." Olare leaned back and then stared at the rocks above him, "Just take care of others here and yourself first."

"If I don't do anything about your arm, it'll get worse and eventually be too late to amputate." Marin said sternly, "Now, stop acting like our father and kindly choose."

Olare glared at Marin and Flick, seeing this chance, spoke, "You never knew about the tunnels under Zanther?"

"Of course, we didn't; you inquisitors did a good enough job at hiding them." Olare looked at Flick, one eyebrow raised, "How familiar are you with them, aside from what we saw?"

"I spent nearly 10 years using them either as a messenger or as an Inquisitor," Flick returned, "I know those tunnels as well as I knew the layout of my estate… And I'm more than willing to share that information with you. I might not have made the choice to follow HaMelech as a knight, but He has called me into His fold and I want to serve you and Him as best I can."

Olare nodded faintly and then gestured a hand towards the second Dove, "Get Flick a parchment and quill. We'll use these tunnels on our next raid-"

"You're not going anywhere until after we return to Apple Ridge, Olare," Marin interrupted as she looked up from her tools, "I want you to get fitted with a mechanical arm, first; I know you can fight without both arms, but after seeing how hard it was on you several days ago, I need to make sure you'll be alright."

Her older brother rolled his eyes and then turned to Flick, "How difficult will it be for my men to find their way through the tunnels?"

That earned a little hum from Flick before he replied, "If they're careful to heed my instructions, and can follow them exactly, they will be safe. Most of the tunnels are marked by nothing more than slightly altered palm prints, so they will need to pay attention to details. However, once they find their way to where they need to go, it's a matter of remembering turns." The former Inquisitor accepted a parchment and quill from the young man Olare had sent away before he began to sketch, "As I said before, they're made to confuse anyone who isn't supposed to be there…"

As Flick spoke, Marin worked at removing Olare's arm. The older man didn't give much of a sign of pain as she worked through the old flesh, though he did grimace the closer she got to the bone. Marin would murmur a sympathetic word from time to time before returning to what she was doing. Flick, meanwhile, did his best to keep Olare focused on something other than his arm being amputated.

When Marin finished, Flick and Olare sat together, quietly, before Rolandus joined. None of the soldiers spoke, though Rolandus did open a flask of wine and pass it between the three of them. Finally, Flick murmured, "So what now? Marin said something about a place called 'Apple Ridge'?"

"That'll be our next stop in two weeks," Rolandus said after taking a drink of the wine, "We'll stay here until then and run a handful of raids on Zanther in order to get our brothers and sisters out before we return. It's a good place to raise a family from what we've seen, and while it might take a moment to get a cottage for you and yours, we'll be able to keep a roof over your head and your family safe. Anca can serve as a Dove with Marin, and you can join us to Zanther or the Bleak Hollow to help pilgrims travel safely. You're a Knight of the Long Road now, friend."

Flick glanced up from the map he was working on to give Rolandus and Olare a smile, "Thank you. It's good to find friends after all that happened in Zanther."

The next two weeks flew by before Flick knew it. He and Anca spent time with the children as they were given broth to their fill, and each night he would lay beside his bride and hold her close- it made him feel like things would be okay as he held Anca near and listened to the fire within the cave crackle.

Drop and Shatter slept for the first three days before they were finally alert enough to sit up and listen to stories as Anca braided Drop's hair and Shatter held onto a small wooden horse that another Kingsman was so kind in gifting him.

When Flick was allowed out of the cave- as his ribs were still healing- he spent time hunting and instructing patrols leaving on how to handle the Inquisitor tunnels. Rolandus kept a sharp eye on him for the first few days before Flick found that he was being allowed to assign patrols and send them out with Olare's permission. He didn't dare go with any, and one of the younger men in the group questioned this, only for Rolandus to reply, "After you have served ten years, risking your life each day, you may do the same."

It was good to know that Rolandus and Olare had his back, and Flick found that he, Anca, and the children were invited to join the two soldiers and Marin for dinner most nights. Over those meals, Flick and the other men would engage in strategizing while Marin and Anca gave their views and opinions on tactics.

Flick also caught sight of Anca slipping out of the cave from time to time to go hunting, though he was unsure of what it was she was doing when she joined the patrols. Rolandus often went with her, though Flick wasn't concerned that the falcon cote would cause problems; he had told Flick that he knew it was not in HaMelech's plan for him to create a family of his own. Instead, he trusted that HaMelech had a family planned in the future that would be established and take him in as a relative despite no relations. Flick didn't understand how he had that faith, but he didn't argue with his newfound friend.

It wasn't until they were nearly ready to go that Anca's secret comings and goings were revealed, "Flick, when the guards found us, they burned everything we had."

"I know…" Flick said, "I was relieved they didn't hurt you more than they did-"

"That included your mantle, and the children's mantles," Anca interrupted quietly, "And I never apologized for losing them."

Flick smiled gently at his wife and kissed her head, "Anca, I'm just glad to know that you and the children are safe. My mantle can be replaced-"

Anca kissed him gently to stop him from talking, "I know, which is why Rolandus helped me make one."

She pulled something akin to a shawl from behind her back, its inky feathers shining iridescent amongst the sunlight, "It's as close as I could get to your original, and I've added a chain to keep it on while you're with the Knights. I'm sorry it's not the same, but..."

Flick stared at the mantle and then at his bride. She was chewing on her lip, keeping her eyes on the ground, when he pulled her into a tight embrace and pressed his face into her hair, "It's perfect, my love... It is better than even my original, and I am so grateful to you for it... When the children are older, you and I can create their new mantles; this is a beautiful one, and I love it."

Anca held onto him, and Flick pulled the feathers over her shoulders to admire them, "You look beautiful in them, as well... Perhaps, once we're settled, we create a matching shrug for you to wear, Mrs. Alastar."

They mounted the rams after the camp was mostly torn down and they rode for three days. They did stop for food and rest, of course, but Flick found that he was growing more and more antsy the longer it took.

Finally, as they reached the crest of a hill, Flick could see a hamlet surrounded by apple trees. Anca leaned out from behind him, her arms around his waist. He could hear the kids laughing as Rolandus told them jokes on the ram next to them while Marin held them near, prompting him to rest a hand on Anca's.

Olare turned slightly to look at them, "It isn't much, but we'll get you a cottage and places to work. There are children of all ages who can play with Drop and Shatter, and we'll be good to you while you gather your bearings to continue to Blackrock..."

"Unless we stay," Flick said quietly, squeezing Anca's hand, "As far as I can tell, this is home until HaMelech says otherwise... and I am more than content with that."

Some stories are stories of luck. Others are stories of fate. This one isn't quite either, as it is a story of faith and love despite a world that seems to be against all things different. And, as Flick held onto Anca's hand and stared down at the village of Apple Ridge, all he could try to do was fathom how he, of all people, had been found and embraced by a God who loved him and his family in a way he would never understand.

About the Author

Ellie Lerum is a prolific fantasy author based in Idaho Falls, Idaho. Inspired by the works of J.R.R. Tolkien, she has carved a niche for herself in the genre of fantastical literature. Her love for writing, reading and blogging is evident in her captivating storytelling. With a dedicated passion for creating otherworldly realms and characters, Ellie has become a figure in the fantasy literary community.

A devout Christian, Ellie's faith has been a guiding force in her writing journey. She draws strength from her beliefs to tackle sensitive topics with empathy and grace, including her personal experiences with pregnancy and miscarriage. Through her writing, Ellie aims to offer solace and hope to readers who may be facing similar challenges.

In addition to writing, Ellie enjoys spending her free time with her family and exploring the great outdoors. She finds inspiration in the natural beauty of Idaho. Her dedication to her craft and her unwavering faith in God continue to shape her work, making her a truly unique voice in the world of fantasy literature.

Also By Ellie Lerum

Jean Cassy 1: Phantom in the Dark
Jean Cassy 2: Souls in the Ice
Tales of Illeross: Gracefully Broken

www.ingramcontent.com/pod-product-compliance
Lightning Source LLC
Chambersburg PA
CBHW061523050726
47503CB00015B/2682